Anyone could see a woman as fine as Karen belonged with a man who had a big future ahead of him....

It wasn't as if Zach had a chance with her. Not a man who'd grown up on the outskirts of town in a rusty old trailer.

He took a ragged breath....

No, he wasn't going to wish, he wasn't going to want.

Some things weren't meant to be.

Zach did the only thing he was allowed to do for Karen McKaslin. He said a prayer for her.

Books by Jillian Hart

Love Inspired

Heaven Sent #143
His Hometown Girl #180

JILLIAN HART

grew up on the original homestead where her family still lives, left home to earn an English degree at Whitman College and later met her husband on a blind date arranged by her best friend. When Jillian is not hard at work on her next story, she reads, stops for café mochas and hikes with her husband in the pine forests near their home in Washington State.

His Hometown Girl
Jillian Hart

Published by Steeple Hill Books™

STEEPLE HILL BOOKS

Steeple
Hill™

ISBN 0-373-87187-2

HIS HOMETOWN GIRL

Copyright © 2002 by Jill Strickler

You should be known for the beauty that comes from within, the unfading beauty of a gentle and quiet spirit, which is so precious to God.

—*1 Peter* 3:4

Chapter One

Karen McKaslin scrambled out of her car in the small back lot behind her coffee shop. The gravel crunched beneath her sneakers as she strolled toward the back steps, squinting against the first fingers of sunlight. Dawn painted the eastern skies with bold strokes of crimson and gold, and larksong merrily drifted on the temperate breeze.

Another beautiful Montana day.

"Hey, Karen!" Jodi Benson called out from the alley as she hurried, the hem of her short skirt snapping with her fast gait. "I heard about you and Jay. How are you feeling this morning?"

"Fine, except that everyone keeps mentioning that man's name." Karen lifted one hand to her brow to shield her eyes from the low glaring sun. "You're late for work, too."

"Don't mention it to my boss, will you? He won't

be in until seven. Hey, don't let this get you down. Every bride-to-be has cold feet. You and Jay will patch things up.''

Not in this lifetime. Karen hiked her purse strap higher on her shoulder. ''Thanks, Jodi. Have a good day.''

Jodi was already at the end of the alley and lifted a hand in answer.

It's not as if they were close friends, Karen thought, so there was no reason to try to set the woman straight. Rumors were rumors and they didn't matter.

She knew the truth, but her troubles felt heavier as she hurried up the back steps. Sweet peas tumbled from the planters on the wooden rail and waltzed with carefree happiness in time with the breeze.

Karen's key clicked in the lock, and she pushed open the glass door with one elbow. She wasn't going to worry about small-town rumors and setting everyone straight, because Jay wasn't her true problem. No, the real problem was before her as she stepped into the little dining room she and her older sister Allison had decorated together.

Today was the third anniversary of Allison's death. Karen had vowed to try to live this day like any other, but at 6:10 in the morning, she'd already failed. She only had to close her eyes to see how this shop looked four years ago when she'd unlocked the door for the first time.

Allison's footsteps had tapped across the subflooring as she'd held her arms wide. ''Imagine all these windows with ruffled gingham curtains. And a counter over there. Our coffee shop is going to be a success, I can *feel* it.''

Karen opened her eyes, the remembrance slipping away, her heart aching. The echo of her sister's voice bounced off the walls, an eerie echo of a memory that felt too real.

Gone were the days when she'd made plans with her sister to run the coffee shop together. Plans cut short by a small-plane crash on this day three years ago. Allison's loss would be forever felt.

Sell the shop, Jay had told her. *When we get married, I won't have my wife working for anyone but me.*

Red-hot rage sliced through her like a sharp blade, and she hated it. Hated both the force of her anger and Jay's unsympathetic demand to sell this place she loved so much.

"Karen?" A man's chocolate-smooth voice broke through her thoughts.

Startled, she spun around. Zachary Drake stood in the doorway, wearing his usual gray Stetson, a white T-shirt and jeans.

Wide and strong and a little rough around the edges, Zach nodded once in greeting. "Standing around daydreaming?"

"Wishing I could pay someone else to get up this early every morning and open for me." She pasted on a smile, since her problems were her own. "You're early today."

"Got a busy morning. Saw you pull in the alley and figured you might make me some coffee even if you aren't open yet." He ambled inside, bringing with him the scent of fresh morning breezes and Old Spice. "So, how about it?"

"For the man who keeps my trusty car running, anything." She slipped behind the counter without another word and stowed her purse.

"Looks like you'll have a busy day, too." Zach couldn't stop his gaze from following her every movement as she broke open a fresh bag of coffee beans. "What with all the tourists dropping by for a cold glass of whatever you've got."

"The tourists are too busy staying on the highway heading for Yellowstone." She flashed him an easy smile, one that didn't reach her beautiful eyes. "Besides, it'll be too hot for anyone to want coffee."

"I might stop by later and get one of those iced things you make."

"That's why you're my favorite customer." Karen grabbed a pitcher of water. "Let me set up and I'll get your cappuccino. It'll take just a minute."

"Appreciate it." Zach turned toward the window, pretending to watch the activity out on the street. Except at eighteen minutes past six on a weekday morning in this small town, there was no activity to watch.

Larks roosted on the edge of the green planter boxes on the wooden rails out front. The streets were empty, and the stores still closed up tight. In the win-

dow of the diner just down the road, Jodi Benson
appeared and turned the Closed sign to Open.

Truth was, he'd rather stare out at nothing because
if he turned around and watched Karen work, she just
might notice the way he was looking at her. Mooning
after her like a man with a secret crush.

Sure, she'd broken off her engagement. Normally
a man might take hope in that. But Zach knew, figured like everyone in this town, that Karen and Jay
belonged together. Whatever had torn them apart a
month before their wedding would be easily fixed, he
was sure, and the two would marry at the end of the
summer.

He could deal with that. His heart took a blow
every time he talked with her, every time he saw her.

"Here you go. One cappuccino, double shot." She
set the paper cup on the counter and held up her hand
when he reached into his back pocket. "No, I don't
have my till set up yet, so don't worry about it."

"I'll catch up with you tomorrow."

"I'm real worried." She flashed him a smile, a
friendly one that had entranced him since his first day
of kindergarten. She leaned both elbows on the
counter and studied him for a moment. "Can I ask
you for a favor? I know you said you're busy, but
could you possibly find a spare minute to take a look
at my car?"

"You mean that rusted-out rattletrap you drive?"

"That rusted-out rattletrap is paid for, cowboy.

That's how I can afford the luxuries of being self-employed.''

"Sure, you can't afford a vehicle that runs."

"Hey, my car runs. Sometimes." She lifted one shoulder and made an attempt at a smile.

"Since I'm the only mechanic in town, I guess the real question is, can you afford to have me look at it?"

"Now you're getting greedy."

"Lots of folks accuse me of that." He winked. "But for you, being my favorite customer, I'll make an exception."

"Oh, boy," she teased back, but the sadness in her eyes remained, dark and steady.

And he knew why. He didn't know if he should say anything. Didn't know if bringing up the subject of her sister would give her more pain. Comforting her...well, it wasn't his right. That right belonged to the man whose ring used to sparkle on her left hand, a small diamond on a gold band.

"I'll come over and take a look when things get slow. On a hot day like this, I never know if I'll be bored to death or if radiators will be boiling over all around town."

"I'm running late. I've got to get in the back and start the muffins baking. Thanks again, Zach."

"No problem." He watched her move away, heading toward the kitchen with ease and grace, leaving his heart hammering.

Longing filled him, and he controlled it. He didn't

want her to suspect how he truly felt. Not today of all days, with the memory of her sister's death and the pain of her breakup written on her face.

Zach grabbed his cup of coffee and headed out into the morning. The sun didn't seem quite as bright.

Thank heavens for a busy day, Karen thought as she laid two slices of bread on the cutting board. A few hours ago, a tour bus had limped into town, blowing blue smoke out the back. The stranded senior citizens had divided themselves between the coffee shop and the town's diner. Add that to the regulars and she could hardly make sandwiches fast enough.

"How are you, dear?" a kindly woman asked from the other side of the counter. "I heard about the breakup. You look like you didn't get a wink of sleep last night."

Karen reached for the mustard jar and slathered a knifeful on both slices of bread. "I'm doing fine, Mrs. Greenley, and don't believe those rumors you're hearing."

"I never do. Just don't you worry about what people are saying. What matters is doing what's best for you." The older woman turned around in line. "Helen, come up here and take a look at your granddaughter. She appears exhausted to me."

"I'm not exhausted." Karen layered ham and cheese slices on top of the mustard-coated bread.

There was a shuffle in the line, and Karen saw Gramma elbowing her way up to the counter.

Great, just what she needed—the woman who could see past her every defense.

Karen concentrated very hard on laying thick slabs of fresh tomato and crisp lettuce leaves just so, before she sliced the sandwich in half. "Gramma, I'm fine. Go back to your place in line. You're cutting."

"I'm doing no such thing," Gramma protested, causing a louder ruckus as she pushed her way to the edge of the counter and circled behind it.

Karen laid the sandwich neatly on a stoneware plate and set it on top of the glass barrier. "And, no, I don't need any help."

"Hogwash. Nora's right. You're as pale as a sheet, and the only place I've seen dark circles like that is on a raccoon. You need to hire help so you can take a day off now and then, missy," Gramma admonished as she grabbed Nora's five-dollar bill and marched to the cash register. "Now, go. Scoot. Nora and I will cover the rest of the lunch crowd."

"You bet," Mrs. Greenley said eagerly. "I've made a sandwich or two in my time."

"There's no way." Karen shouldered against her grandmother and counted out change from the till. "I'm perfectly fine. Make yourself a sandwich, go sit with Mrs. Greenley and have a good visit."

"You can't fool me, sweetie." Gramma's arm settled firmly around Karen's shoulders. "Use that line on someone who hasn't been around as long as I have. You haven't been sleeping."

"I have a long line of customers—"

"*Karen.*" Gramma's voice was firm but caring. "I don't know all that's going on between you and Jay, but I'm on your side. Never forget that. And I know what day it is. Allison would want you to visit her, you know."

"I can do that later—" Karen turned away, hating that Mrs. Greenley had stepped behind the counter and was taking the next order. "I can't afford to pay you—"

"That's good, because we're volunteering." Gramma gave her a grandmotherly shove toward the door. "I know, it goes against your grain to accept help, but you're always doing for others, Karen. Don't deprive me of the pleasure or I'll drag you to my Ladies' Aid meetings for the rest of the year."

Suddenly the shop was too loud. The clatter of plates, the scraping of silverware and the cackling din of voices all scraped over Karen's raw nerve endings.

A hand closed over hers, one whose touch was dear and loving. "Sweetheart, let me finish up for you."

"No, I'll be fine." She *would* be fine.

"Go outside and get some air. Give yourself all the time you need. Nora Greenley, I can't read your chicken scratch on this ticket. Does that say turkey and Swiss?"

"Of course it does," Nora answered back, digging through the commercial refrigerator. "See? I told you that you need new bifocals."

"That's the *last* thing I want to hear." Gramma

grabbed a pair of plastic gloves from the box on the counter.

Just like that, Karen was superfluous in her own business.

"Hey, are you all right?" someone asked. A hand lit on Karen's arm, the touch warm and caring.

"No, Julie, I just need some air." Stumbling away from her friend, Karen headed straight to the back, threading around customers and cloth-covered tables to where sunlight glinted on the glass door.

Her hand hit the brass knob and she sprinted into the hot sunshine.

Hot aching tears that wouldn't fall turned the world into a blurred mass of green, blue and brown as she tripped down the walkway, running her hand along the banister so she wouldn't lose her way. A nail head gouged into her skin and pain jolted through her palm. She felt the wet sting of blood and dropped to the stairs, burying her face in her uninjured hand.

Mom was tumbling into another bout of depression and it seemed like nothing could stop it. The coffee shop was on the brink of disaster—the shop her sister had loved. And she'd just broken her engagement to a man her parents practically worshiped. She couldn't stop the weight of failure pressing like a thousand-pound rock on her chest.

Worst of all, she still missed Allison with a fierceness that nothing could erase. Not time. Not grief. She'd lost her best and lifelong friend and even now she felt as if she had no one to turn to.

"Hey, it looks like you need a handkerchief." A rugged male voice broke through her thoughts.

Zachary Drake settled onto the step beside her. Grease smudged his cheek and was smeared across the front of his otherwise white T-shirt.

He certainly was a handsome man. Her heart kicked at the sight of him. He looked tough as nails, as if growing up the way he had could never quite be taken out of him. But she knew Zachary Drake was as strong and dependable as the day was long.

He pressed a folded handkerchief into her hand. Only then did she notice that her car's hood was up. He'd been taking a look at the troublesome engine and she hadn't noticed him.

Ashamed and embarrassed to be caught crying, she rubbed the cloth across her eyes and down her face, wiping away the wetness of her tears. "Don't tell me you have bad news about my car."

"Okay, I won't." He caught hold of her right wrist. His touch was hot and unsettling. "You're bleeding."

"It's nothing serious."

"I'm not too sure about that. Looks like a lot of blood to me." He stood and strode down the steps, his big body moving with an athlete's power and ease. He disappeared in the shadow of his tow truck, parked behind her car in the alley.

She heard the click as he opened his truck's door and the crunch of his gait on the gravel as he returned.

Even without his motorcycle, which he frequently rode through town, Zach still looked a little untamed as he'd always been in school. Maybe it was the way the wind caught his dark hair and whipped it across his brow, or the slight swagger to his walk.

"Let me clean this up and we'll see who's right— if it's nothing or not." He knelt before her, opened the first-aid kit on the step between them and reached for her injured hand.

At the first touch of the gauze to her cut, she winced.

"Sorry about that. It's got to hurt."

"It does," she lied, because that was the easiest explanation. She felt jumpy, as if every nerve had been laid open from his touch.

It's only Zach, she told herself. I've known him forever. But her heartbeat picked up as he leaned closer, his fingers a warm touch on her skin.

He swabbed the blood away from her cut with careful brushes of the sterile gauze. Each swipe was gentle. Soon he'd exposed the two-inch gash along the side of her palm.

"See? I was right." His words were a smile of victory, but his gaze felt like something else, something deeper. "This is going to require some expert care."

"You're a *mechanic,* Zach, not a doctor."

"No, but I get a lot of scrapes, so I know how to take care of them."

"That makes you an expert?"

"It ought to make me something."

"Clumsy?"

"Watch what you call me. I'm the only mechanic

around, and let's face it, Karen, if your car's any indication, you need me. Badly.'' He dug through the small plastic kit and produced a sealed packet of antiseptic.

The air caught in her chest when he leaned even closer and rubbed the salve across the tear in her skin. Like a bee's sting, sharp pain traveled the length of her cut. ''I hate to break it to you, but you'll never be a doctor. That hurts.''

''Is that so?'' He lifted one brow as he laid a butterfly bandage across her wound, his voice warm with teasing. ''What are you? A wimp who can't take a little pain?''

''Thanks. I suppose you're one of those tough guys who never admit to a weakness like pain.''

''You've got that right.'' He tore open another package and removed a bandage, a wide pad that covered her entire wound. His fingers were a warm pressure in the center of her palm as he made sure the adhesive stuck. ''There. An expert repair job.''

How could it be that she was smiling? The weight on her chest remained, but it was easier to breathe, easier to find a way to face what she had to do. All because of Zach. ''Now I owe you two favors.''

''Good. I like it when pretty women are in my debt.'' He snapped the kit closed.

When he straightened, unfolding his six-foot frame, he towered over her, casting her in shadow. The sun gilded his hair and the width of one shoulder. The wind caught in his brown locks and tousled them.

He held out his hand. "You look like a woman who needs a friend. Lucky for you, I just happen to be available."

"Is that so?"

"Absolutely."

Karen fit her good hand to his. Her pulse jumped, leaving her shaken.

Normally when she was with Zach, she didn't react like this. But today, everything was off balance. She didn't know what was wrong with her.

"Thanks, Zach." The words caught in her throat, and the lump of tears was back, thicker and hotter than ever. "I appreciate the patch job. Now tell me what's wrong with my car."

"I'm still working, but I can tell you it looks like a cracked head. We're talking about a whole new engine."

The strength went out of her knees and Karen leaned against the banister post. She stared at her poor car.

A new engine. There was no way she could afford that. No way at all. "It's still working, right? How much longer can I drive it?"

"Hard to say." Zach raked one hand through his thick hair, stepping closer, casting her in his shadow again. "I'd say you have anywhere from an hour to a week. It just depends. I can find you a rebuilt engine if money's a problem."

"Money's a problem." This was the *last* thing she needed. "Are you sure it doesn't need a new belt or hose or anything cheaper?"

"I'm sure. I can order a rebuilt engine and have it here in a couple of days. Since you're my favorite customer, you wouldn't have to pay for it all at once. I trust you."

"A dangerous move. I could be a bad credit risk. I've got a balloon payment on the building coming up at the end of next month." Karen sighed, feeling the weight of stress clamp more tightly around her chest. "Even if I scrape everything together to pay for it, it'll be tight for a long time."

"I know what that's like." He lifted a big round car part from the ground and dusted it off. "Take some time to think about it and let me know if you want an estimate."

She looked at the raised hood of her poor car and the grease-coated engine beneath. "How long will it take you to get all these parts back where they belong so my car's running again?"

"Ten minutes tops."

"I have a few errands to do. I'll be back. Thanks again, Zach."

"That's what I'm here for. Hey, Karen, are you going to be okay? Do you want me to call someone for you? Your grandmother or your sister Kirby?"

"No, I'm fine." She had to be. She had no other choice.

But she suspected Zach didn't believe her as she hurried down the alley.

She didn't believe it herself.

Chapter Two

An emergency call came when he was finished with Karen's car. The early '70s model with a rusting olive-green paint job managed to start after several attempts. There was no doubt about it—the car needed serious help.

He shut off the ignition, tucked the spare key back into place behind the visor and climbed out into the scorching sunshine.

Karen's scent from her car seat—a combination of baby shampoo and vanilla—clung to his shirt. A sharp ache of longing speared through him, old and familiar, and he ignored it. Over the years he'd gotten good at ignoring it. The scent tickled his nose as he ambled across the gravel lot. He ignored that, too.

The coffee shop looked like it was quieting down. The group of tourists must have headed out, now that their bus was as good as new. He didn't have time to step inside and wait for Karen to get back from her errands, not with an elderly woman's radiator boiling over in this heat.

There was nothing else to do but to hop into his truck and let the air-conditioning distribute the faint scent of vanilla and baby shampoo.

Great. That was going to remind him of Karen for the rest of the afternoon.

When he'd been patching up her cut, he'd been close enough to see the shadows in her dream-blue eyes. He hated that there wasn't a thing he could do to comfort her.

Anyone could see a woman as fine as Karen belonged with a man like Jay, a man with a big future ahead of him. And even on the off chance that Karen didn't marry Jay, it wasn't as if Zach had a chance with her. Not a man who'd grown up on the outskirts of town in a rusty old trailer.

He took a ragged breath, vowing to put her out of his mind. He checked for traffic on the quiet street and pulled out of the alley.

As he drove down the main street, he saw Karen coming out of the town's combination florist and gift shop. His pulse screeched to a stop at the sight of her. She didn't see him, walking away from him the way she was, so he could take his time watching her. Karen was fine, all right, and as beautiful as a spring morning. Head down, long light brown hair tumbling forward over her face, she carried a live plant that was thick with yellow blossoms.

No, he wasn't going to wish, he wasn't going to want.

Some things weren't meant to be.

Zach headed the truck east away from town and did the only thing he was allowed to do for Karen McKaslin. He said a prayer for her.

Karen watched as her gramma's spotless classic Ford eased slowly into the cemetery parking lot. The rumble of the engine broke the peace of the late afternoon.

She stood, squinting against the brilliant sun, and left Allison's flower-decorated grave. She waited while her grandmother parked her car and then emerged, clutching a bouquet of white roses.

"I recognized your rattletrap of a car in the lot." Gramma held her arms wide. "How's my girl?"

"Fine. I'm just fine." Karen dodged the bouquet and stepped into her grandmother's hug. More warmth filled her, and all the worries bottled up inside her eased. "I shouldn't have left you with the shop like that. I shouldn't have let you bully me."

"You were powerless to stop me." Gramma stepped away, squinting carefully, measuring her with a wise, sharp-eyed glare. "Don't try to fool me, young lady. You don't look fine. You look like you're missing your sister."

"She was my best friend."

"I know." Gramma's voice dipped, full of understanding. "Let me go set these on her grave. She loved white roses so much."

Tears burned in Karen's throat, and it hurt to remember. She remained in the shade of the oaks, so that her grandmother would have time alone at Allison's grave.

Karen watched as the older woman ambled across the well-manicured grounds, through lush green grass and past solemn headstones.

Sorrow surrounded this place, where bright cheerful flowers and a few colorful balloons decorated graves. At the other end of the cemetery, she could see another family laying flowers on a headstone in memory.

Time had passed, taking grief with it, but Karen didn't think anything could fix the emptiness of Allison's absence in her life or in her family. Not time, not love or hope.

She waited while her grandmother laid the flowers among the dozens of others. She waited longer while the older woman sank to her knees, head bowed in prayer.

In the distance, a lawn mower droned, and overhead, larks chirped merrily. It was like any other summer afternoon, but this day *was* different.

"Now that I've given thanks for the granddaughters I still have, I'm ready to go." Gramma took Karen's hand. "I closed the shop for you, so there's no sense hurrying back this late in the day just to open it for an hour. Why don't you come home with me and give me a hand?''

''You know I can't say no to you.''

''Good, because I promised your mother that I would make sure supper's on the table tonight, not that anyone will feel much like eating. But since she's my daughter, I'll do whatever she'll let me do. And if that's to make my famous taco cheese and macaroni casserole, then so be it.''

''What about Mom? Dad's busy with the harvest. Maybe I should run home first and see how she is. Make sure she isn't alone.''

''One of your sisters is with her—Kirby, I think. I called from the shop before I came here.''

Karen felt the sun on her face, the wind tangling her hair and the disquiet in her heart. So many responsibilities pulled at her, but she could feel her grandmother's love. Because they were standing in a cemetery with both life and death all around, she nodded, unable to say the words.

There was never enough time on this earth to spend with loved ones. It was a truth she couldn't ignore, not after losing Allison. Time was passing even as she let Gramma lead her toward the parking lot where their cars waited in the shade.

''Do you need me to stop by the store and pick up anything?'' Karen asked as she opened her car door.

''I already did. No grass grows under these feet,'' Gramma answered, her blue eyes alight with many emotions.

Karen's throat tightened, and she climbed into the driver's seat. Even with the windows rolled down to let in the temperate breezes, she could still smell the scents of mechanic's grease and Old Spice, evidence of the man who'd sat behind this wheel only hours ago.

A rumble of a powerful engine drew her attention. In her rearview mirror she caught sight of Zach's blue-and-white tow truck rolling up the driveway.

She turned the key in the ignition and gave the gas pedal a few good pumps, and the engine started and died. Started and died. Started and coughed to life. Gramma was parked at the edge of the lot, patiently waiting.

Karen put her car in gear and pulled around, having only enough time to wave to Zach as he rumbled into one of many empty parking spots. He lifted a hand in return. The tips of yellow blossoms waved above the dash, and she sped away, somehow touched beyond words.

She knew without asking that he'd brought flowers for her sister's grave.

"Is this why you asked me over?" Karen turned to her grandmother the minute she stepped foot inside the kitchen door. "Don't tell me you've taken up Mom and Dad's cause?"

"What cause, dear?" Gramma set her purse and keys on the nearby counter.

"Trying to show me how wrong I am to call off

my wedding.'' Trying to control her anger, Karen pointed at the sunny picture window. Over the top of the short cedar fence, she could see Jay mowing his mother's lawn next door. ''I'm not going to be pressured about this.''

''I'm not trying to pressure you.'' Gramma circled around the polished oak table and headed for the refrigerator.

''No, but silence speaks volumes.'' Karen turned her back on the window. She wouldn't let the guilt in. ''You think I'm going to forgive him and marry him anyway, just like Mom does. Like everyone does.''

''I respect your choice, either way.'' Gramma set two cans of diet cola on the counter. ''Of course, Jay *is* awfully handsome. He's dependable and easy on the eyes.''

''He doesn't love me, Gramma.''

''Then why on earth did he propose to you?''

Karen didn't answer. She couldn't admit the truth. If Allison were alive, she would have been able to confide in her, but who else would understand?

Karen watched as her grandmother calmly scooped ice into two glasses. She worked methodically, easily, content with the silence. Tall and slim, she looked comfortable in her usual flowered dress and low, sensible shoes.

''Sit down.'' With a clink Gramma set the glasses on the round oak table and looked through her glasses perched on her nose. ''Tell me all about it.''

"About what?"

"What's taken away my favorite granddaughter's smile."

"I don't want to talk about Jay." Karen pulled out a chair and settled onto the cushioned seat. "Or how I'm looking thirty in the face and don't have any better prospects."

"Fine. Then we won't talk about Jay." Gramma took a sip of soda, understanding alight in her eyes. "Most of my friends have great-grandchildren by now. Nora was one of the last holdouts. Then her granddaughter married Matthew and got those triplet boys. I don't suppose I'm going to be that lucky."

"Don't count on it. I see where you're going with this. You're trying to get me to talk about my breakup with Jay."

"Not at all. I'm just sharing some of my troubles with you for a change. At my last Ladies' Aid meeting, Lois had new pictures of her adorable great-granddaughter."

"You're feeling left out. Is that it?"

"Yes, but you don't look very sorry for me."

"Sure I am. I'm hiding it deep inside."

Gramma's eyes twinkled, full of trouble. "If you went ahead and married Jay, then in a year or so I'd have my own great-grandbaby to show off. I've got to keep up with my friends."

"I see. It's a status thing. Like having a new car or the right house?"

"Exactly."

Karen ran a finger through the condensation on the outside of her glass. "Jay has one semester left at seminary, and then he wants me to sell the coffee shop."

"Why is that?"

"He needs me to help him with his career. A pastor's wife belongs at her husband's side, he told me. Then he asked how much equity I had in the building."

"I see." Gramma nodded sagely. "You and Allison opened that shop together. It would be hard to sell just for the money."

"I got angry and so did he. He said some harsh things—" She took a deep breath. "He told me the real reason he wanted to marry me. Because I was someone he could count on. I work hard, I know how to run a business and I'm comfortable, like an old friend. He needs someone dependable to help him with his career."

"I see." Gramma lowered her glass to the polished table. Ice cubes clinked in the silence between them. "Those words must have been hard to hear from the man you loved."

"I was in love with him."

"Not anymore?"

"How can it be love, if he doesn't love me back?" Anguish filled her. "Everyone tells me I'm wrong. I should be lucky to have a man like Jay who wants to marry me. He's going to go far, and he'll be a good husband."

"They don't know the real story, do they? You haven't told this to anyone but me."

"Not even Mom." Karen let out a shaky sigh. She'd never felt so confused in her life. "I don't know what to do. Am I wrong? I love Jay—at least a part of me did—and is that enough? Do I settle for friendship? Or am I throwing away something good? It feels as if I've done the right thing and the wrong thing all at the same time. You were married to Granddad for thirty years, so tell me what you think."

"I know one thing." Gramma reached across the table and her warm, caring hand covered Karen's. "Love without passion is like lukewarm water. It's not good for much."

"Then you think I did the right thing?"

"I think you should do whatever makes you happy. Forever is a long time with a man who doesn't love you the way you want to be loved."

Some of the weight lifted from her chest, and Karen managed to take a sip of soda. "I thought you wanted great-grandchildren."

"I want my granddaughter to be happy. That's more important to me than anything in this world, even keeping up with Lois." Gramma's fingers squeezed gently, a reminder of the love Karen had known her entire life. "It's tough when the man you're interested in thinks you're a cup of lukewarm tea. I have the same problem with Clyde."

"Clyde Winkler, the man you've been seeing?"

"You look surprised." Gramma took a long sip of

her cola. "What? You don't think a woman my age can have a love life, is that it?"

"I'm speechless."

"And do you know what I've figured out? Men are all the same. They haven't changed a bit since 1940. Still as thickheaded as ever."

"Surely not every man in existence."

"The one I'm interested in, at least." Gramma stared out the window, where the drone of Jay's mower grew louder, then began fading away. "I'll tell you something I've never told a living soul. Once, I was in the same situation you're in."

"You called off a wedding?" Karen leaned closer. "With Granddad?"

"I almost did. I was younger than you are now, but back then, girls married much younger. All my friends from school had husbands, and I desperately wanted to get married. More than anything. Oh, what plans I had! I wanted a house of my own, children to raise and a man to take care of."

"Which you did. Granddad was wonderful."

"But he wasn't the love of my life." The confession was a quiet one, hardly loud enough to be heard above the hum of the air-conditioning.

Karen dropped her glass. Ice cubes and soda sloshed over the rim and onto the table.

Gramma calmly reached for the napkin holder and began mopping up the mess. "Surprised you, didn't I?"

"But you loved Granddad. I know you did. I saw you together."

"I did love him in a hundred different ways. As my husband, as the father of my children, as my best friend. But not in the most wondrous way. He never said, but I know that he felt it, too. He tried and I tried. While we made a life together, we lacked something important." Gramma rose and dropped the wet napkins in the garbage container. "We didn't have a deep emotional connection. That was something we couldn't make together, no matter how hard we tried."

I don't believe it, Karen thought. Denial speared through her. Her grandparents had always been happy together.

No, *seemed* happy together, she corrected herself. And as she watched her gramma's shoulders slump and felt the truth in the air, Karen realized the pain her grandmother must have silently lived with every day of her marriage.

When Gramma straightened, what looked like sadness and regret marked her face. "Your granddad told me once that he was glad to be with such a reliable woman. That out of all the women he could have married, he'd been lucky to wind up with me.

"Reliable." Her voice shook a little. "I loved Norman deeply, but not deeply enough. Just as he could never love me. Even now I wonder what it would have been like for us if we'd managed to figure out

what we were missing. We were never really happy.
We were never truly unhappy. Lukewarm.''

Karen stood and paced to the window. She could
see Jay in his mother's backyard, pushing the mower.
Tall and dependable, he was a handsome man with
golden hair and sun-bronzed skin. The faint growl of
the engine rumbled through the glass, and looking at
the man whose ring she'd worn made sadness weigh
on her heart. "Granddad wasn't your true love."

"I made a life with him and it worked out fine. I
was blessed. I won't say otherwise." Gramma
paused, letting the silence fall between them. "But a
woman yearns to be something more than 'reliable'
or 'comfortable' to the man she loves."

Karen turned from the window, relief filling her.
"That's the real reason why I broke the engagement.
It wasn't only about the coffee shop. He doesn't really
love me, so how will he feel about me in ten years?''

"Love *can* grow and deepen with time." Gramma
slipped an arm around Karen's shoulder. "But there
are never any guarantees. Are you having regrets?''

"I know I hurt him. He's a fine man, but he's not
the right one. I've prayed and prayed over it. Mom
thinks I'm being foolish. But you don't.''

"No, I don't. Did the Lord answer your prayers?''

"No. No confirmation either way.''

"You're a good girl. God will answer you. Be pa-
tient.''

"See, that's my problem. I'm not good. I'm just
average.''

"Average? My granddaughter? Nonsense." Gramma marched Karen to the table and gestured for her to sit. "You are a bright, beautiful young woman and as good as can be. I ought to know, since I'm your grandmother. A woman my age is wise about these things."

"You're biased."

"I guess love will do that." Gramma ran her fingers through Karen's brown hair. "Do you know what I think?"

"I'm afraid to guess."

"You might look good as a blonde. Ever think of that?"

"What do you mean? Color my hair? What does that have to do with this conversation?"

"You'd be surprised." Gramma looked up into the mirror on the wall behind the kitchen table. "I've been thinking about getting rid of this gray hair. Maybe that's my problem. If I dyed my hair red and bought a sports car, I wouldn't be the same old reliable Helen."

"You wouldn't be the grandmother I know and love."

"I'm not getting any younger, so why wait? And at my age, what am I waiting for? I want something different than spending most of my days in this lonely house. I want to know passion in my life. That's what I want."

Karen twisted around in her chair, surprised at the unhappiness etched on her grandmother's face.

"You and I have the same problem, Karen. We've been good girls all our lives and in my case, it's been a few decades too long."

"What do you mean?"

"I've been living a lukewarm life for sixty years now, and that's not how I want to be remembered. I don't want people to say, 'Helen was nice,' at my funeral. I want them to say, 'Remember the fun we had the day Helen drove us through town in her new convertible.'"

Karen's hand trembled, and she didn't know what to say. Today at the cemetery, she'd felt the same—that time on this earth was too short to spend with regrets.

Sympathy for her grandmother filled her. "If you want, I'll go with you to the beauty shop. We'll get your hair done so you'll look beautiful."

"Thank you, dear. I knew you'd understand." Gramma held her close, and Karen hugged her long and hard, grateful for this grandmother she loved so much.

Chapter Three

Karen was placing fresh flowers on the tables in the quiet hours before the lunch rush started when an engine's rumble on the street outside her shop caught her attention. A gleaming black motorcycle pulled into an empty parking spot out front, ridden by a man wearing a white T-shirt and jeans.

"There's trouble," matronly Cecilia Thornton, Jay's mom, commented over her iced latte.

"With a capital *T*," Marj Whitly agreed.

With the way Zach's muscled shoulders and wide chest stretched out that T-shirt, there was no word other than 'trouble' to describe him. Karen watched him swing one leg easily over the bike's seat and unbuckle his helmet. Shocks of thick brown hair tumbled across his brow.

Zach might look larger than life, but she knew at heart that he was a good man.

He strolled down the walk in front of the row of windows and winked when he caught sight of her. Eager for the sight of a friendly face, Karen quickly set the last little vase in the center of the last table.

The bell above the front door chimed. Zach strode through the door. Her pulse skipped and she didn't know why.

"Working hard on a Saturday, as usual. Don't you know you're missing a fantastic morning out there?" Zach raked one hand through his tousled locks, rumpling them even more. He lowered his voice. "I'd offer you an escape on my bike, but I don't think Jay's mom will approve."

"You noticed her glaring at you?" Karen circled around the counter.

"Always." His eyes sparkled, holding no ill will toward the woman who frowned at him from the far corner of the dining room.

"Is it too early for lunch?"

"Not in my shop."

"Then I'll have a bologna and cheese with mayo and mustard, on white." Zach nodded in Cecilia's direction. "Good morning, ladies."

The two women's eyes widened in surprise. Cecilia managed a polite response, even though it was clear she didn't approve of the likes of Zachary Drake.

See? With that kind of attitude in Jay's family, it was a good thing she'd broken her engagement.

Zach leaned over the counter, a mischievous grin

curving across his mouth. "I don't think they approve of my mode of transportation."

"It's not the bike, Zach."

"Are you saying those woman don't approve of *me?*"

"You're crushed, I see."

"Devastated. Is Cecilia's death-ray glare of disapproval getting to you?"

Biting her bottom lip to keep from laughing, Karen donned clear plastic gloves. "Cecilia's death-ray stares aren't hurting me any. I missed you this morning. You didn't come in for coffee. Are you two-timing me over at the diner?"

"I wouldn't dream of it. I'm a devoted man. Not even the diner's full breakfast menu can tempt me away from your charming shop."

"A loyal customer. Just what I like to hear."

"I have to confess I made my own java and took a thermos of it fishing with me this morning."

"I didn't know bachelors could make coffee."

"You see, there's this little scoop that comes in the can. It's easy to measure."

"A can? You didn't even grind your own beans?" Karen unwrapped a loaf of fresh bread. "I'm disappointed in you."

"I know, but I've learned my lesson. Next time I'll bring my thermos over and let you fill it for me."

How did he do it, she wondered. With that dazzling smile and his melting-chocolate voice, Zach could chase away her troubles and leave her smiling.

"How's that car of yours?"

"Still running, and don't look so surprised."

"Only prayers are keeping that heap going, believe me. When it finally breaks down for good, give me a call and I'll help you out."

"Unlike you, I have complete faith."

"Unlike you, I've looked under the hood, and that car's doomed, Karen. I'm telling you this as a friend. I've already ordered a used engine."

"I can't afford it."

"We'll work something out or we can barter. Car parts for sandwiches?"

"That's a lot of sandwiches."

Zach sent Cecilia a brief, imposing glare. "Mrs. Thornton still hasn't forgiven you for dumping her son?"

"Does it look like it?"

"If she's upset, what's she doing in your shop?"

"This is the only place in town to buy a latte." Karen sighed.

"You're doing the right thing, giving it time." He meant to be comforting. "Everyone knows you and Jay will get back together."

"Everybody doesn't know me, not if they believe that. I'm never going to marry Jay." Karen concentrated extra hard on her sandwich making. "I suppose that's what you think, too, isn't it? That good, dependable Karen will do what's sensible. And why not? It's what I've always done."

"That's the problem with a small town. People

make up their minds about what kind of person you are, and it doesn't matter how honest you try to be when it comes to their repair bills, they still see what they're used to seeing."

"I know what you mean." Karen's pulse skipped again. Had Zach's eyes always been so blue? "Have a good afternoon."

"Good luck surviving Cecilia's death-ray stare." He tossed a five-dollar bill on the counter and took the paper sack from her.

His hand brushed hers and burned her like a hot flame.

Why was she feeling like this? Confused, she watched Zach push open the door, causing the bell to jangle overhead. For a brief moment he glanced at her, his eyes dark with unmistakable sympathy.

Then he turned and was gone. The bell chimed again as the door snapped shut, and Karen felt as if all the warmth had gone from the room. What was wrong with her? What was going on?

She didn't mean to be watching him, but there he was. Striding down the walk with the wind tousling his dark hair. He looked as rakish as a pirate, and yet as dependable as the earth. He hesitated at the top of the stairs and then he disappeared from her sight.

Caffeine, that's what she needed. Karen reached for the pitcher of iced tea and poured a tall glass. The sweet cool liquid slid down the back of her throat, but it didn't ease the confusion within her.

The bell chimed again. Zach—had he come back?

Karen held her breath as the door swung open to reveal not her handsome mechanic but someone just as welcome. Her grandmother swept into the room wearing a red T-shirt, a pair of denim shorts and tennis shoes.

Karen nearly dropped her glass. "What happened to you?"

"I raided Michelle and Kirby's closets. I've been wearing dresses all my life. It's time for a change." Gramma set her purse on the counter. It was a neat slim red pocketbook instead of the sensible black handbag she always carried.

What was going on?

Gramma faced the dining room and clapped her hands. "Ladies, Karen sure appreciates your business, but she's going to have to close up shop for a few hours. I know you understand. Here, Cecilia, let me get a paper cup so you can take your latte with you."

Cecilia's disapproving glare gained new intensity. "Helen, whatever have you done to yourself?"

"What? A woman can't wear shorts in the heat of summer?" Her grandmother looked nonplussed as she transferred Cecilia's latte from the mug to the paper cup. "Now, head on out so I can lock the door."

"Gramma!" Karen stepped forward before her grandmother took over completely. "You can't do this. It's nearly time for the lunch crowd."

"But you have to leave right now." Gramma flipped the sign in the window so it read Closed. "It's the only time Dawn over at the Snip & Style could fit us into her schedule.''

"What do you mean by 'us'? *You're* the one getting your hair colored. I'm going for moral support. That's what we agreed to.''

"That's not how I remember it. Come on, get your keys. I'm not about to be late, not when Dawn has promised me a whole new look.''

"Gramma, I'm glad you're doing this. I'm thrilled, really. But lunch brings in the biggest sales of the day. I can't miss it. Maybe Michelle can—''

"Your sister has a client scheduled—you. I mean it, ladies, out of those chairs. Hustle.'' Gramma gave a good-humored clap, looking as if she were herding reluctant deer from her rose garden. "Thanks, ladies. Karen sure appreciates it.''

"Anything for our Karen,'' Marj Whitly said warmly. "That's just the thing she needs, Helen. Time for herself at the beauty parlor, a complete shampoo and facial. Restores the spirit, it does. Then she'll be over her wedding jitters and can get down to the business of marrying your son, Cecilia.''

Karen opened her mouth to protest, but Gramma winked at her, so she offered Marj a lid for her cup instead.

Gramma locked the door after the women departed. "Leave your purse. This is my treat.''

"What treat? I'm going to say this one more time so you understand. I'm going along for moral support *only*.''

"Of course you are," Gramma said indulgently. "Now get a move on, because I don't want to be late for my new life."

See? This is what always got her into trouble. In the end, she hadn't been able to disappoint her grandmother. Look what that had gotten her.

"It wasn't supposed to do this," Michelle, her youngest sister, apologized. "Working with hair is always tricky. You have a lot of naturally gold highlights in your hair, which was a surprise considering it's such a dull brown—"

"I never should have agreed to this." Karen wished she had Cecilia Thornton's knack for a death-ray glare. "I should've never trusted you."

"I guess I left the color in too long."

"You *guess?*" She could only stare in the mirror at her wet, scraggly hair. It hung in limp, ragged strands and shone perfectly gold. Except in about ten or twelve places. "Look what you did to me. My own baby sister."

"Sorry. This is the first time I've ever turned someone's hair green. Honest."

"Fix it. Whatever you have to do, do it now."

Michelle grabbed a fresh towel. "I know what to do. I think."

"You *think?* What did they teach you at that school anyway?"

"They warned us never to work on our own relatives. Now I know why." Michelle dashed away and disappeared from sight.

"It's certainly different, I'll grant you that," Gramma said from the neighboring chair. "With those green streaks, you could be in the latest fashion. Anywhere but in Montana."

"Thanks, I feel so much better." Karen peered at her reflection, her heart sinking. What if Michelle couldn't fix it? "I didn't mind being mouse brown. At least my real color wouldn't glow in the dark."

"That's the spirit. Don't worry. We'll turn you into a dazzling blonde yet. Michelle might be new at this, but Dawn here has decades of experience. She can work wonders. Why, look at me."

"I'm looking." Karen couldn't believe her eyes as the other beautician switched on a blow dryer and began styling Gramma's hair.

No more gray curls. Rich auburn locks fell in a short, feathery cut. She looked beautiful. Infinitely beautiful.

"I've always wanted to be a redhead," Gramma confessed above the hum of the dryer. "It's a whole new me."

"You don't need any improvement." By contrast, Karen's hair looked like a cosmetology school disaster. "Look at me. I could sure use something. Michelle, I want you to put this back the way it was."

"Don't be silly," Gramma admonished. "You promised moral support, so don't think I'm going through this alone. You're staying at my side every step of the way, missy. It'll be good for you.''

''I don't want a makeover.''

''You need one more than anyone else I know, my darling sister.'' Michelle returned, armed with a cup that smelled like varnish. ''I don't know how it happened, but you got all the recessive genes in the family. A shame it is. Gramma, you wouldn't know a good plastic surgeon, would you?''

''Mess up my hair again, and you'll pay,'' Karen threatened.

Michelle didn't look a bit afraid. ''I know you too well. You're all bark and no bite. How about platinum blond streaks? What do you think, Gramma?''

''No! No streaks. No blond anything.'' Karen couldn't help panicking a little. ''I've come to adore mouse brown. Really. It's the way God meant me to be. Just give me a rinse or something to get this color out of my hair.''

''Trust us, Karen.'' Gramma winked. ''They say that blondes have more fun. Let's find out if it's true.''

Seeing the happiness on her grandmother's face, how could she refuse—even if disaster loomed?

Zach felt the hot midday sun burn the back of his neck as he twisted the bolt with his pliers. ''Your car should start fine, Mrs. Greenley.''

''You, my dear boy, are nothing short of an angel.''

The older lady blew him a kiss. "Tell me why a handsome man like you doesn't have a ring on his finger."

"No girl can catch me, I guess." Zach shut the car's hood.

"Doesn't a smart fellow like you know not to run too fast?"

He wiped the grease smudges from his fingers off her gleaming hood. "No one said I was a smart man."

"You can't fool me, Zachary Drake." Nora Greenley shook her head at him, watching every movement he made as he reached around the steering wheel and turned the key. "You're not as bad as you seem, even with the motorcycle. How much do I owe you?"

The engine rolled over, purring contentedly. He released the key. A movement caught his gaze on the sidewalk across the street. Karen with hair as gold as summer sunshine breezed out of the Snip & Style. She looked more beautiful than he'd ever seen her.

Then he remembered Mrs. Greenley was watching him. Anyone with good eyesight would be able to see how he felt for Karen, so he closed his mouth and turned to his client. "I'll bill you for the battery. Have a good afternoon."

"I'll sure try." The older woman glanced across the street before she climbed behind the wheel. "You behave yourself, you hear, young man?"

Zach closed Nora's car door and waited until she pulled away. Alone, he dared to look across the street again. There she was, with her grandmother at her side, talking with a group of women who'd spotted them on the sidewalk. Their conversation rose and fell with merry energy, but all Zach could see was Karen.

She looked great as a blonde. The lighter color made her eyes bluer. Somehow it made her seem more wholesome, if that could be possible, as if she'd spent all summer outdoors in the sun.

Karen's words from earlier in the day echoed in his mind, replaying over and over again. *Everybody doesn't know me, not if they believe that. I'm never going to marry Jay.*

Words like that could give a man hope.

Home. Finally. Zach snapped on the light switch just inside the door of his apartment over the garage. A bulb popped with a bright flash, leaving him in darkness.

Great. Just great. Too exhausted to even summon up a little anger, Zach rummaged around in the dark. His closet was too messy and so he couldn't find his flashlight. His stomach grumbled in loud protest, not wanting to wait a second longer for supper. He'd change the bulb later and make do with the light in the kitchen.

Sweat trickled down the back of his neck, and he tugged off his T-shirt. Man, it was hot. He headed straight for the air-conditioning window unit and flicked it on high. Tepid air sputtered reluctantly, and the fan inside coughed. A lukewarm current breezed across his heated face.

What? No cold air? He flicked off the machine, marched across the small apartment to the kitchen and yanked open the window above the sink. Humid air blew in. As he circled his apartment, opening the windows wide, his stomach clamped with hunger.

Food. He needed it bad and he needed it now.

Not overly hopeful, Zach scoped out his kitchen cupboards. At the sight of the practically empty shelves, his stomach twisted harder. A can of olives, a stale box of cheese crackers and there was mold growing on the remaining slices of three-week-old bread.

Okay, maybe the refrigerator held more promise. He jerked open the door and stood in the welcome icy breeze, surveying the empty metal racks. There was only a half-empty jar of mayonnaise, the butter dish and an empty container of salsa. His stomach growled so loud, it hurt.

Maybe there was something in the freezer.

Bingo. He'd found supper. Even if it was two beef franks, heavily iced in their original package stuck to the empty ice tray, which was iced to the bottom of the freezer. This was not a problem—he was ingenious and he had a knife.

Using it like a chisel, he inserted the blade's tip between the thick bed of ice and the frozen franks. Cold air wheezed across his face as he leveled a careful blow.

The phone rang—the shop phone. It was work and he couldn't ignore it. Reluctantly he set down the knife and knocked the freezer shut with the flat of his hand. A meal, air-conditioning and time to relax— was it too much to ask?

He grabbed the old black phone in the corner by the door.

"Zach's Garage." He tucked the receiver between his ear and his shoulder.

"I know it's late." Karen's voice came across the line, tight with strain. "But remember that offer of help you made? I could really use it."

"You called the right man. Don't tell me your engine went and died, just like I said."

"Okay, I won't, but that's why I'm calling." Static crackled across the line. "No one at home is answering the phone. They're probably outside on the deck, so I'm stranded. I'm at the grocery store."

"I'll be right there."

"Thanks, Zach."

"No problem. That's what friends are for." He eased the receiver into the cradle and grabbed his keys.

Dinner could wait. Relaxing could wait. Karen needed him. Even if it was only as a mechanic, only as a friend.

He grabbed a clean shirt before heading out the door.

He spotted her sitting on the curb the minute he turned onto Railroad Street. The night breezes ruffled her silken hair around her delicate face. Her slender shoulders slumped with either exhaustion or defeat. He couldn't tell which.

She turned at the sound of his truck and waved. Behind her, the lights of the closed grocery store were dim and cast a faint glow over her, emphasizing her willowy shape. She stood, holding a plastic grocery bag in one hand.

He stopped the tow truck in the middle of the road and leaned out the window. "Hey, good lookin'. Need a lift?"

Her new blond locks danced against the side of her face, driven by the wind. "Do you like the new me?"

"There was nothing wrong with the old you." He reached for his door to climb down and assist her, but it was too late to help her in. She was already breezing through the beams of the truck's headlights, so he leaned across the seat and opened the door. He gave it a shove for her because it was heavy. "What's with Helen? I saw her new hairdo."

"Gramma is having a midlife crisis three decades too late."

"Good. Everyone needs to try something new now and then."

Flashing him a grin, Karen climbed inside the cab as if she were used to climbing into big trucks. And then Zach remembered she was a ranch girl and had probably helped her father in the fields through the years by driving hay trucks and tractors.

What would it have been like to grow up as she did, with a solid and close-knit family and hundreds of acres of land to roam on? It was a far cry from living at the edge of town where he'd called a single-wide trailer home. And where he'd struggled to take care of his younger brother and sister.

The bench seat dipped slightly with her weight. The air-conditioning circulated her vanilla and baby shampoo scent. Yes, a man had to have hope. That's all it was—hope—and not the right to be more than a friend.

Not knowing what to say, Zach released the clutch. The truck eased down the street in a smooth rumble.

He headed north, away from the lights of the small town where rolling fields stretched into the deepening twilight. The roar of the engine and the whir of the cool air through the cab covered up the silence that fell between them. But it didn't change the fact that she was sitting next to him with only two feet between them.

Yes, it was good for a man to have hope.

"What are you looking at?" she asked, her hand flying to the sassy ends of her hair. "You hate this, don't you? I can't get used to looking at myself."

"Neither can I." He fought the urge to tell her just how great she looked. He thought her beautiful before, but she looked better now. Not because her hair was different, but because there was a sparkle in her eyes he hadn't seen in a long while.

"Gramma forced me into this."

"She strong-armed you, did she?"

"She guilted me into it. Works every time." Karen

shook her head and her jaunty locks swept her slim shoulders. "I'm a soft touch when it comes to her."

"When it comes to everyone."

"Sometimes." She looked unhappy, and he never much thought about the pressures she might face always looked to as one of the well-behaved McKaslin girls, even now when she'd been an adult for many years.

"I have the same problem," he confessed with a grin. "I'm always a real softhearted guy. That's why I drive my motorcycle through town at least once a week. So no one suspects the real me."

"It's a good disguise. It fools a lot of people, but not me."

"Really? Maybe I shouldn't have left the leather jacket at home." He tossed her a grin as he slowed down to turn into her family's long gravel driveway.

How she liked Zach's smile. Kind and warm with a hint of charm, and when his smile touched his eyes, she could see the goodness in him. In fact, there was a lot to like about the man.

Aside from being a dependable friend, he was probably the most handsome man in town. He'd certainly been considered the best-looking boy in her high school class. All the years since had only improved him.

Even in the dark interior of the truck and silhouetted by the encroaching night, he looked amazing. His profile was strong with a dark shock of hair tumbling over his forehead, a straight nose and a well-carved jaw. Just looking at him made her pulse drum.

Zach slowed the truck down to take the final corner of her parents' long gravel driveway. She looked through the windshield and saw her family's home up on the knoll. The lit windows shone like beacons in the descending darkness.

The truck eased to a stop in front of her house, and the silence between them lengthened. Light from the house spilled through the open windows to cast a glow on the trimmed juniper bushes lining the driveway.

She didn't want to walk through that door. The pressure of her parents' disappointment in her pressed like an anvil against her chest.

"I can take that in if you want." His voice startled her, and his big warm hand curled over hers.

His heat seared her like a jolt of electricity and she jumped at the contact. Then she realized he wasn't trying to hold her hand. He was taking the plastic bag from her grip.

To her amazement, he opened the door and hopped from the cab. His boots crunched in the gravel and then tapped on the brick walk. The light from the windows burnished him with a golden glow. His silhouette was impressive—broad shoulders, wide back, tapered hips and long legs.

He was all male, that was for sure. Hard and strong and powerful. Something she'd never quite noticed to this degree before.

Her heart kicked for some unexplained reason, and she fled into the fields where the darkness swallowed her. She knew every bump in the dirt path that led from the house to the stable.

She splayed both palms on the worn smooth curve of the top rail and let the calm of the night surround her. Dark clouds blocked out the stars. She didn't know how long she waited before she heard Zach's gait on the path behind her and felt his presence, substantial like the night.

"Karen? I'll head back to town and rescue your car. I can have an estimate ready for you sometime tomorrow."

"There's no hurry. It's not like I can afford that engine."

"Stop being so difficult. In my book, you're a good credit risk. Besides, you've got a business to run. You need your car."

"I do." Trying not to give in to her troubles, she took a breath and let the wooden rail take the weight of her head. Too late—her neck muscles had coiled into one hard aching mass.

Gathering her hair in her free hand, she held it up in a loose ponytail so the winds could caress a warm current across her knotted muscles.

His work boots tapped behind her. "A little tense?"

"That's an understatement."

"Let me see what I can do about that."

She felt a swish of air over her exposed skin and

then his warm fingers settled on her neck. She stiffened at his touch, but the heat of his palm felt like heaven.

A sigh escaped her as his big, callused hands caressed and soothed the pain from her muscles. Her tension melted with every glide of his fingers over the back of her neck.

Too soon he stepped away, leaving her breathless. His touch was like nothing she'd known before—electrical and enlivening and comforting all at once.

She was grateful for the dark. She didn't know what to say, and even if she did, how would she say it?

As if he were flustered, too, Zach walked away without saying a word.

The thick blanket of clouds broke apart overhead, and thin, silvery moonlight brushed the ground where Zach walked. A verse from Matthew came to her as soft as the breeze. *"…and He will give you all you need from day to day."*

There was no doubt about it. She was blessed with Zach for a friend.

She stepped into the swatch of moonlight and began jogging to catch up with him. "Hey, where do you think you're running off to? Did you get supper?"

"No. I was in the middle of chiseling frozen hot dogs out of my freezer when you called."

"*Chiseling?* Unbelievable. I've heard bachelor stories before, but I didn't think they were true. Even my father can cook well enough to make an omelet in a pinch.''

"I've been busy. I didn't have time to get to the grocery store.''

"Sure, a likely story." She met him halfway across the yard. "Zachary Drake, you're pathetic, but I can't in good conscience let you starve.''

"Pathetic? C'mon, give me a break, I'm not that bad. Usually.''

"Sure, like I believe you." She led the way up the brick steps and onto the porch. "A man who thinks crusted-over hot dogs is a worthy meal is a danger to himself.''

"Does this mean I'm in luck and you're going to feed me?''

"Somebody's got to.''

He laughed, a rich, wonderful sound that warmed her all the way to her soul.

Chapter Four

❧

The microwave beeped and Zach watched Karen pop open the little door. The light inside snapped on to reveal the sight of a steaming cheesy casserole. It made his mouth water.

"That's the best thing I've seen all day."

Karen smiled breezily. "If you're really nice to me, I'll give you the recipe. If you can fix a car, you can learn to make this."

"That's a bet I'm not willing to take. If I could cook as good as I can build a transmission, my stomach wouldn't be growling. I haven't had a decent meal since my little sister left for college."

Karen set the plate on the kitchen table. "What have you been eating for the last year?"

"They have these boxes in the freezer part of the grocery store. I buy 'em, take 'em home, and when

I'm hungry, put one in the oven. They're called frozen dinners.''

"Shocking." Teasing glints lit her eyes and chased away the worry lines across her brow. She tugged flatware from a nearby drawer and set a knife and fork on the table. "Sit. Eat. It's a wonder you haven't spontaneously combusted with all the chemicals you've been ingesting."

"It's not that bad. They've got these healthy frozen meals that taste pretty good. But nothing like your grandmother's cooking."

"I won't argue with you about that." Karen set two soda cans on the table. "Go ahead and get started. I'll dish up a nice bowl of salad."

"You're going to torment me with vegetables?"

"Even a man as handsome as you needs his antioxidants."

"Antiwhats? That sounds suspicious. Let me guess. It has something to do with broccoli."

She peered around the edge of the refrigerator door. "What's wrong with broccoli?"

"It tastes like cellophane, for one thing. As a general rule, I never eat anything green."

"It's a wonder you've made it this far, Zachary Drake. A tough guy like you needs his vitamins." She shook her head, golden locks shimmering as she shut the door. "I've got a bowl of carrot sticks. Do me a favor and eat a few. Hey, don't look at me like that. They're orange, not green."

"Orange is a good color. Lots of junk food is orange."

She rewarded him with another smile, one that chased away all the shadows from her eyes and the strain from her face. A smile that made her look like the Karen he remembered. Happy and wholesome, with the kind of beauty that settled in a man's heart and never faded.

Those are dangerous thoughts, Zach. He tried not to notice the way his skin felt prickly when she sat down beside him.

He bowed his head in a quick prayer and reached for his fork.

Delicious spices and creamy cheese melted across his tongue. "This is great. I'm so grateful, I'm liable to give you the engine you need for free."

"Don't you dare, although Gramma will appreciate the compliment." Karen popped the top of the cola can and sipped.

No ring sparkled on her finger. He couldn't forget what she'd told him. That she wasn't going to marry Jay. *Ever.*

Hope was a bright blessing as the night darkened and he could see his reflection in the white-paned glass of the kitchen's bay window. And of the woman sitting next to him, her bouncy hair sparkling like pure gold, her presence as sweet as the cut roses scenting the air.

This was definitely something he could get used to.

Forget coming home to an empty apartment and eating alone in front of the TV.

A door opened behind him and the hot, evening wind whipped across the back of his neck as Karen's mother and grandmother entered the kitchen.

"Mom." Karen bolted out of her chair and circled around the table, her arms extended.

Zach watched as she wrapped her mother in a comforting hug. Mrs. McKaslin looked frail and ashen, but when she glared at him over Karen's shoulder, she looked as tough as nails.

Mrs. McKaslin didn't need to say the words. Zach had lived with the same looks from half the town since he was a boy—looks of disdain and judgment. Looks that said he wasn't quite good enough, even twenty years later. He'd worked hard to become a man of integrity, but he was still Sylvia Drake's son from the wrong side of town.

"I'm in the way here, Karen." He grabbed his empty plate and carried it to the sink. "Let me rinse this off and I'll be on my way."

"What? No seconds?" Karen released her mother and moved to stop him, her beauty just as bright and her friendship as genuine. "Let me grab the casserole from the fridge and I'll dish you up another—"

"I'm good, Karen. Thanks anyway."

"You haven't had dessert yet."

Mrs. McKaslin's gaze grew sharper, and Zach could feel the man he was fade a little. "It's getting late."

"Are you sure? Mom, would you mind wrapping up a few of your brownies? If Zach has to go, at least he can take heaven with him." Karen's smile shot straight to his heart.

She was heaven.

Good thing she couldn't read his thoughts. Embarrassed, he set his plate in the sink.

"Oh, no, you don't." Karen sidled up to him and curled her hand around the hot water tap. "I'd still be sitting on that lonely sidewalk if you hadn't shown up tonight. Thanks, Zach. I owe you big-time."

"Pretty lady, you don't owe me a thing."

Her soft mouth stretched into a quiet smile. She smelled like heaven. He wanted to breathe her in, wrap his arms around her and pull her against his chest.

He'd give about anything to have the right to hold her.

"Karen." Mrs. McKaslin cleared her throat from the other side of the room. "It's been a very hard day for me. I want my bath now."

Strain tightened in the corners of Karen's eyes and mouth, stealing away her beautiful smile. "I'll be right there, Mom."

"Nonsense. I can do it," Helen called out and set a paper sack on the counter. "Zach, don't forget to take this with you. A man can't live without a dose of my double-chocolate fudge brownies. I sprinkle them with powdered sugar just to make them sweeter."

"Thanks, Helen." He took the carefully folded sack and avoided Karen's gaze. "Karen, I know you're busy. I can find the door on my own."

"Don't you dare." Her hand brushed his arm as she escorted him from the room.

He could feel Mrs. McKaslin's prickly gaze on his back, and he tried to ignore it. Karen walked quickly beside him, and without a word pulled him through the foyer toward the front door. Her shoulders looked tight and a muscle jumped beneath the smooth skin on her jaw.

"I'm sorry about my mother. She's battling depression again and it turns her into a harder person."

"Hey, I'm fine. I'm sorry that she's not feeling well." He felt sorrier for Karen.

The phone rang in the kitchen behind them as he pulled open the elaborate front door. "Now that your car is dead, just like I predicted, will you need a ride to town tomorrow? I could be bribed into swinging by to pick you up."

"I'll take Mom's car." Karen's hand settled on his forearm, light and steady. "I can't begin to tell you what your friendship means to me. If I didn't know better, I'd think you're an angel in disguise."

"Me? The last time I looked, angels don't ride Harleys."

"There's a first time for everything." She pressed a kiss to his cheek, warm and sweet, just like her.

Friends. He didn't miss the message in the words.

She wanted friendship with him, not romance. His hopes fell like a star from the sky.

Tucking away his disappointment, he stepped into the shadows.

She stood bathed in the gentle glow of the overhead light, and there was no mistaking the grateful gleam in her eyes. She watched him not with attraction or interest or affection. But with gratitude.

"See you tomorrow," he said, a dutiful friend and nothing more. "Thanks for supper."

Before she could answer, Mrs. McKaslin's voice called from inside the house. "Karen, honey, it's Jay on the phone. He's waiting to talk to you."

Zach was glad the shadows hid him from Karen's sight. "Sounds like you'd better take that."

He walked away and didn't look back. He was halfway to the truck when he heard the door close with a quiet *click,* leaving him alone.

On the outside.

Just like always.

Footsteps tapped in the dark aisle behind her and tightened her grip on the currycomb. The stall was shadowed, lit only by the moonlight that cut through the top half of the open stall door. She couldn't see who was heading toward her. Star shifted, her hooves clomping on the concrete floor, and cut off Karen's view of the door.

"It's me," Michelle said quietly, pain in her voice.

"I got Mom to take a sleeping pill and stayed with her until she fell asleep."

"I'm glad she's resting." The mare she was brushing nickered low, as if in comfort, and Karen leaned her head against the old horse's warm shoulder. "I shouldn't have made her so angry."

"You didn't want to talk to Jay. You had every right to refuse to take his call." Michelle paused, as if she had something on her mind and decided not to say it. "Tomorrow will always be better. At least, that's what Pastor Bill says."

"Tomorrow is almost here, and I have to get to bed." She felt weary all the way down to her soul, but she feared another sleepless night was ahead. "You go on back to the house. I'll be up in a few minutes."

"Okay. I just wanted to make sure you weren't still mad at me. About the green hair, I mean." How unsure Michelle seemed, her voice thin, clinging to the shadows.

"I could never be truly mad at you. You're my baby sister."

"If you want, I can give you back your dull, mouse-brown lifeless color. That is, if you don't like the golden beauty you've become from my expert touch."

"Expert touch? Ha!" Karen meant to tease, but her heart weighed down her words.

She wrapped her arms around her sister, frail-boned like a colt still growing, and hugged her long enough so there could be no doubt the hair disaster was forgiven.

What blessings she had in her sisters and in every aspect in her life.

"Hey, Karen." Michelle halted at the moonlit doorway. "Wake me up when your alarm goes off in the morning. I'll drive you to town and help you at the coffee shop before church."

"*You?* Help? You don't know the first thing about a kitchen. I'm afraid you'll burn the place down."

"Just keep me away from all electrical appliances and I'll be fine."

"Then it's a deal. See ya in the morning."

"How much are you going to pay me per hour?" Michelle asked, her teasing as bright as the moon. "What? You think I'd do that for free? No way. I need the cash. I've got a lifestyle to maintain."

As her sister disappeared into the night, Karen was laughing for the first time since she'd refused Jay's call and disappointed her parents even more.

Maybe now they believed her that there wasn't going to be a wedding.

Tonight, her future seemed empty. She didn't know what was in store for her.

Help me please, Father. I'm trying, but I just can't hear Your will for me.

No answer came to her. Star nudged her hand in a show of comfort, a reminder that she wasn't alone. Even when it felt that way.

* * *

"Hunky Zach's at the front door." Michelle wandered into the coffee shop's small kitchen, a mop in hand. "Should I do you a favor and let him in?"

"Absolutely. He may have news about my car." Karen slipped the last pan of muffins onto the oven racks.

"I figured you might say that. He's too handsome to leave out on the street, isn't he?" Michelle winked, laughing. "Are you actually blushing?"

"It's the heat from the oven," Karen explained as she closed the door gently.

"Sure." Michelle stole a fresh muffin from the cooling racks. "I'll help myself to breakfast and you answer the door. He wants to see you anyway."

"Hey, leave my muffins alone." Karen set the timer. "Did you finish mopping the floor like I asked?"

"Are you kidding? What do I look like? A manual laborer?" Michelle leaned against the counter and peeled back the paper baking cup.

"No, but you do look like a freeloader who's eating my profits for the day."

"Well, I *did* get up early to drive you this morning. You ought to at least feed me."

"What am I going to do with you? When the buzzer for the next batch rings, will you take them out?"

"I can do that." Michelle picked out the raisins and flicked them into the garbage bin across the room.

"Oops, I missed that one. Don't worry, I'll pick it up."

"Don't burn my muffins," Karen warned as she found the courage to leave her little sister to watch the oven. Which was probably a big mistake.

Her sandals tapped an echoing rhythm through the dining room, but the noise was nothing compared to the thump of her heartbeat when she saw Zachary Drake standing on the other side of the glass door.

It ought to be illegal to make men that exquisite. The morning breeze tangled his dark, unruly hair. Today he was dressed for church. A dark jacket shaped his magnificent build and tan pants encased his long, lean thighs.

Why was she noticing?

She opened the door to the scent of Old Spice. "Don't you clean up nice."

"I try. You aren't looking so bad yourself." His gaze slid lazily from her French-braided hair to the tips of her sandals. He quirked one brow. "Blue toenails?"

"Thanks to Michelle." She gestured to the kitchen door where her little sister was spying on them. "Gramma and I had the complete works over at the Snip & Style. Even a pedicure."

"At least your toes match your dress. Not everyone in church will be able to say that."

"Lucky me. Can I get you something to eat? I have blueberry muffins ready to come out of the oven—"

An alarm in the kitchen buzzed and Michelle reluctantly tore herself away from her spying duties. "They're ready right now. Come and join us."

"How can I say no to that?" Zach reached into his pocket and handed her a slip of paper. "I've got your estimate. Like I said, the engine's ordered. I can get started in a few days. Be done by the end of the week."

Karen stared at the precise numbers in the bottom right-hand column. She didn't need to ask Zach to know he'd given her a discount. And probably had charged very little for his labor.

It was still more than she can afford. "I can't pay for this. Maybe you could hold off for a couple of months. Let me make my balloon payment and see if there's anything left over."

"We've already discussed this. You pay me when you can." He ambled across the dining room. "In exchange, you'll let me help myself to those delicious-smelling muffins."

"I'm not putting a strain on our friendship because I owe you money."

"Like I would want you trying to get by without a working car? C'mon. I'm a better friend than that." He flashed her a dazzling wink before he stepped into the kitchen and out of her sight.

Why was she noticing that his wink was dazzling? Or how strong he looked when he crossed a room, all man and might and charm?

She was *not* attracted to him. Not a chance. It was caffeine deprivation, that was all. Because after the royal mistake she'd just made with Jay Thornton, she'd wasn't about to turn around and make another one.

Besides, romance was the best way to mess up a good friendship.

"Michelle, is that pot of coffee ready?" Karen snapped the front door shut, making sure the lock caught, and resolved to solve her caffeine-deprivation problem immediately. "How are the muffins?"

"Yeah, yeah" came Michelle's response through the open door. She sounded very distracted.

Karen knew why. Michelle was leaning against the counter again, picking at her muffin, gazing at handsome Zach as if he were Mel Gibson.

Apparently Michelle was coffee deprived, too. Maybe all men looked better right before a jolt of caffeine.

Well, that was easy enough to fix. Karen grabbed three paper cups and reached for the steaming carafe. She poured with unsteady hands and sloshed coffee over the rim of one cup.

"These are good. Thanks." Zach held up one of two muffins he'd pilfered from the cooling racks. "They'll keep my stomach from growling during the service."

"Unlike last time?" Karen teased.

"I'm on my best behavior today because I'm hoping that you two lovely ladies will accompany me to church. I always show up alone and that's why I can't get any dates. I don't look desirable."

"You? Desirable?" Karen took a big sip of coffee.

"See? I get that all the time. Girls always see me as good old dependable Zach. The guy who helps them when their cars break down. That's all. They can't see that beneath the engine grease and the tough-guy mechanic's image, I'm a heck of an eligible bachelor. A real catch."

"You're a real something, that's for sure." She laughed, reaching for a muffin. "I don't think Michelle and I can do anything to help *your* sorry image."

"Sure you can. Other women will see you two clinging to me, and they'll get curious. I'll have them flocking around me in no time. It's the least you can do for me." He nodded toward the written estimate she'd laid on the counter. "Since I'm giving you a line of credit."

"You drive a tough bargain and I'm in no position to argue. But sitting next to you in church with adoring looks on our faces? Do you think we can stand it, Michelle?"

"Oh, I don't know." Michelle shook her head, feigning disdain. "It might ruin my reputation as the best beautician in town. People might begin to question my sense of taste and style and flock to Bozeman for their cuts. Dawn would fire me."

"Exactly." Karen turned off the oven and removed the last batch of muffins. "My customers will migrate to the diner across the street. I'd be destitute."

"You girls sure know how to deflate a guy's ego."

He fought to keep from chuckling. "Okay, new deal. Sit with me, but no adoring looks. I'll survive. I'll never meet a woman, fall in love and marry. One day I'll be known to all as the old man who fixes cars and who can't cook for himself."

"Everyone has their crosses to bear." Karen tried not to laugh, shaking so hard with the effort that a muffin tumbled from her fingers.

Zach scooped it from the floor. "Tell me you won't put this on the discount display?"

"No, that's only the day-old stuff." Karen unplugged the coffeemaker. "Everything that falls on the floor I save for you."

Zach's laughter filled the room, echoing warmly as Michelle flicked off the overhead light. In the darkness, his hand lighted on her shoulder, just for a moment, and his breath was warm and pleasant against her ear.

A friend, that's what he was. That's all he was, even if she couldn't help noticing him.

I need more caffeine, she thought, glad she'd brought her coffee with her.

"There you are. Knew you'd be behind this counter. You sneaked out of church before I could grab you."

Karen took one look at her sharp-eyed grandmother as she marched past customers in the crowded coffee shop. "Hey, what do you think you're doing back here?"

"Helping out my granddaughter." With a twinkle in her eye, Gramma stashed her purse next to the sink and turned on the faucet. "Thought I could make myself useful."

"You should be over at the café with your friends for Sunday brunch."

"The truth is, I need you to do a favor for me. So I figured I would do one for you first."

Words of doom. Karen sliced the sandwich she was making down the center and placed it on a plate. "What kind of favor?"

"A big one. One a loving granddaughter does for her grandmother, no questions asked."

"I was afraid you were going to say that." She rang up the sale at the cash register and counted back change. "No, Gramma. Whatever it is. I've lost enough business this week, taking a whole afternoon off to turn my hair green."

"This is the Lord's day. They'll be no talk of profit and losses. Besides, I'm only asking you to close early." Gramma winked, and only then did Karen realize how beautiful she looked with her tasteful auburn curls and a breezy summer dress.

"Is that Mom's?" she asked.

Gramma's eyes sparkled her answer as she stepped up to the counter. "Why, hello, Julie. Don't you look pretty today? What will you have?"

"The special, please." Julie Renton, one of Karen's close friends from high school, lifted a brow in a silent question.

Karen shrugged, whipped up an iced mocha and rang up the sale.

"Watch out. Jay just walked in," Julie warned in a whisper as she slipped a five-dollar bill onto the counter. "I noticed you managed to avoid him at church."

"If only I could be so lucky now." A heavy weight pressed down on her chest, making it hard to breathe, but Karen found solace in her friend's sympathetic smile. She counted back change. "Thanks for the warning."

"I'll try and head him off." Julie dropped a dollar in the tip cup and headed toward Jay.

"Need one of those iced tea things," Gramma called from the counter. "Mr. Trouble here says he wants something cold."

"Mr. Trouble?" Then she spotted Zach at the head of the line. "Hi, stranger. Wait, I don't see any women flocking around you. I guess Michelle and I didn't help your image like you thought we would."

"You two didn't cling and adore me, remember, so none of the other women got jealous. No one even noticed me."

"Well, you'll have trouble getting anyone in town to do that." Laughing, Karen grabbed a wide-necked bottle of raspberry-flavored tea from the commercial refrigerator and set it on the counter by the till. "Don't even think of paying for this. It's on me."

"Now, I didn't mean—"

"It's *my* treat today," Gramma cut in and handed

the generous sandwich to Zach. "He's going to be doing me a favor, too."

"That's news to me." Karen frowned. Just what was her grandmother up to? "Would you mind enlightening me?"

"Not at all, dear. Let's just wait until the rush dies down and I'll tell you all about it. Don't go hounding Zach for any answers, because I've sworn him to secrecy."

"Sorry, Karen." Zach turned away. "I can't break my vow to a lovely lady like Helen."

Gramma looked innocent as she took the next order.

"I know what this is about," Karen whispered to her grandmother as they made sandwiches side by side. "You're going to pay for my car repairs, aren't you? Just like you tried to do last time."

"What? Me? Waste money on that worthless rattletrap?"

"You've tried to do it before, and I know what you're capable of." Karen swabbed mayonnaise across the bread. "I don't want your money. The haircut was enough. Will you promise to keep your wallet in your purse?"

"Fine. I promise."

"That was too easy. Wait, you're scheming and don't deny it." Karen layered the meat with garnishes, then sliced the sandwich in half. "Tell me the truth. What's this favor you want from me and Zach?"

"Oh, it only involves a quick trip to Bozeman."

"Bozeman? I've got my business to run, and after I'm done here I have to head home. Mom couldn't get out of bed to make it to church and I'm worried—"

"Your sister Kirby will be at home with her. Don't forget that you promised to help me."

"I did. I'm just worried what's next."

Karen finished a second sandwich, laid them on plates and grabbed soda cans from the refrigerator. As she rang up the purchases, she spotted Jay next in line. Tension knotted in the back of her neck.

"Hi, Karen." He stood arrow straight and rigid, looking as tense as she felt. And just as hurt. "That's great Helen's here. She can take over for you. Come and talk to me."

"There's nothing to talk about. You know that."

"I want to find out what happened. I know what you said, but you couldn't have meant—"

"I meant it, Jay. I don't want to marry you." Sadness filled her, looking at this man she'd once made dreams with, at the man who couldn't love her.

He'd never love her, not truly. He saw her as a practical choice for his future, that was all. He'd never be able to give her the depth of love she wanted from a husband.

She knew he'd never be able to understand how a practical sensible girl like her would want true love.

"Did you want to order? Today's special is Swiss and turkey—"

"C'mon, Karen, don't be like this. I've got a flight to catch in a few hours. Didn't you listen to Bill's sermon today? It was about letting go of our grief and moving on. Of accepting that God's plan may differ from what we wish for ourselves—"

Karen felt her grandmother's curious gaze and realized their conversation wasn't as quiet as she'd thought. She lowered her voice. "I know you don't love me. Marriage should be about love. Are you going to order or not?"

"No." Jay drummed his fist on the glass counter, rattling utensils and drawing surprised gazes from several diners.

Flushed, he marched toward the door.

He was a golden son of this town, a man destined to be a great minister. Next to him she felt plain as she always did, plain and small.

Because that's how he saw her.

She was doing the right thing. Certainty filled her and all her turmoil faded away like fog to sun.

Gramma wrapped her arm around Karen's waist. "You did good, my girl."

"Not really." Karen leaned into her grandmother's embrace, grateful for the comfort and for the blessing of this woman in her life. "I'm finally at peace over this."

"I'm glad. I finished filling the last order, so let's treat ourselves to some lunch. I'm in a hurry to get to Bozeman."

Karen reached for two slices of whole wheat bread. "What's in Bozeman? C'mon, tell me."

"I certainly will not. You'll just have to wait and see for yourself."

Karen felt a strange heat, as if someone were staring at her. She looked up, expecting to see Jay's mom and her death-ray glare of disapproval.

Instead, she saw Zach. Seated across the length of the dining room, he winked at her.

The peace in her heart intensified, and she swore that sunlight streamed through the windows, brightening the room.

Chapter Five

The late-afternoon sun beat relentlessly on the paved lot outside the car dealer's office. Karen had to squint against the bright rays to see her grandmother emerging through the glinting glass doors.

"She's all mine!" Gramma had never looked so happy as she approached the shining red convertible, jingling brand-new keys. "I can't believe it. This is a dream come true."

"A beautiful dream. One I hope you share now and then. I'd love to go joy riding with you." Karen wrapped her grandmother in a hug. "You're going to look like a new woman in that car."

"Don't you know it." Gramma beamed. "And yes, I'll treat my granddaughter to a drive, but not right now. You've got to take Zach back to town for me. After all, he did negotiate the price of the car. I can't let him walk home."

"I guess not." Karen considered the man who stood talking with a salesman in the shade of the building. He'd changed into his usual white T-shirt and jeans. With the wind tangling through his dark locks he looked fine.

Very fine.

"I suppose I can tolerate his presence for a little longer, but I'll need the keys to your old Ford."

"It's not mine any longer."

"Gramma! You traded in that car? You've had it for as long as I can remember."

"I had it brand-new off the showroom floor since long before you were born. It's been my only car for nearly forty years. Forty years! And it never broke down on me once and left me stranded. A blessing, that Ford is, and that's why I'm giving it to you."

"What?"

"I have an extra car, and you don't have one."

"I do, too. It's in Zach's shop waiting for a new engine."

"That old rattletrap? It breaks down once a week. Why would you sink perfectly good money into a wreck like that?"

"Because it's mine and it's paid for. Thank you, but no. I can't take your car. You should hold on to it. It's a classic and—"

"I've made up my mind and I'm not changing it. I'm giving the car to you." Gramma's hand closed over Karen's. "You work too hard, harder than most, and you deserve a little help."

"No, I don't need—"

"You're a good girl for wanting to pay your way, but indulge me. Take my car and consider it a favor for your doting grandmother."

"It's an entire car. It's worth money."

"Money I don't need. I've spent my whole life scrimping and saving. It's time I loosened my belt just a little. Life is too precious not to enjoy, and I get happiness from helping my grandchildren.

"So here." Gramma pressed the keys against Karen's palm. "Drive home that helpful young man who got me a fantastic price for my new roadster. And treat him to dinner because he's a man and they just don't know how to take care of themselves."

"I don't know what to say. It's an entire car. One that runs. 'Thank you' doesn't seem enough—"

"But it is, sweetie. Don't forget what I said. Take Zach out to a nice meal as a favor to me, because I've got plans." Gramma looked so happy as she brushed her hand across the new car's cherry-red fender. "I'm going for a spin in my new convertible. Wait until my friends see this!"

"You be careful in that thing. It goes from zero to sixty in like five seconds or so. You're not used to that kind of power."

"No, but I'm going to get used to it." With a wink, Gramma slipped into the soft-looking leather driver's seat and placed her hands on the wheel. "I'm going to enjoy every second of this. Bye, dear. Thanks for the help, Zach."

Zach nodded goodbye to his friend and stepped into the sunshine. "Helen, you stay out of trouble."

"I'll try." She started the engine with a twist of the key and put the roadster into gear. "Adios!"

Karen watched the little red car with her grandmother inside zip through the parking lot and pull onto the street. "*Adios?* She's never said that before."

Zach watched as the convertible sped out of sight. "I'm glad for her. It's always a good idea to take some time and enjoy this life we're given."

"I could learn from my grandmother's example— is that what you're telling me?"

"Something like that. Let's take a spin in your new old car, and I'll show you what a great machine you've inherited."

"A great machine?"

"That's right." Zach opened the driver side door. "Climb inside and start her up. You're bound to notice the quick start, the smooth shifting and the powerful purr of an expertly maintained engine."

"That's right. You're Gramma's mechanic, too." Karen leaned against the Ford's polished fender. "Sure this is safe to drive? Not that I'm doubting your mechanical abilities, Zach, but my car was always breaking down. And you are always the one working on it. I see a correlation, and it isn't a pretty one."

"Ah, did you notice how I said *maintained?* Not *resuscitated?* There's a difference. Plus, this is a fine automobile.'' Zach held the door wide for her and gestured for her to sit. "It's guaranteed not to break down like your old heap.''

"Guaranteed?" Karen slipped into the seat and reached to adjust it. "Do I have your word on that?"

"Absolutely. I'm an expert, and I'm telling you that this car has a lot of good, trouble-free miles ahead of her.''

Zach shut the door, gentleman through and through. Karen watched him circle around the hood. Being with him made her feel lighter than air, as if all her problems had vanished. The sun felt brighter, the wind fresher as she fit the key into the ignition.

Zach settled on the seat beside her and stretched out his long, denim-encased legs. Nicely muscled, those legs were. Very nice.

And why exactly was she noticing—again? And worse, she was feeling a little woozy. It *had* to be from low blood sugar. She'd had a rushed lunch, and it was nearly dinnertime. "Where do you want to eat?"

"There's a drive-in down the road that serves the best onion rings this side of Missoula.''

"A drive-in? I think when Gramma said she wanted me to take you to dinner, she envisioned something with waiters. Where your salad is followed by a grilled entrée and vegetables.'' She put the car in gear and eased through the lot. "Something healthy.''

"Healthy? You think that's healthy? I don't know

where you get these ideas. Hamburgers cover all the basic food groups—meat, bread, cheese and lettuce. What more could you ask for?''

"I'm speechless. You are logic challenged. That's the only explanation."

"What do you mean? French fries are just cut-up potatoes. It all makes sense. Growing up on a ranch with all those vegetables everywhere has warped your perspective. It's a good thing you've started hanging out with me. I'll show you the right way to eat."

"I'm not sure the nation's nutritional experts would agree with you."

"What do they know?"

She pulled into the small parking lot where a red-and-white sign boasted the best burgers in town. "Doesn't look like they serve salads here."

"That's the beauty of it. The problem with you is that you're too wholesome, Karen. So come with me and live dangerously."

"Eating deep-fried food *could* be dangerous."

"I'm not talking about the food." Zach winked and climbed out of the car.

Karen could only stare at him, unable to move. He'd had her laughing, and now he was causing her to feel something else entirely. Her skin prickled with awareness as he opened her door and held out his hand. He was so masculine, and he made her very aware of being a woman.

When she placed her palm to his, she felt a zing

of energy travel through her. She could no longer deny it.

She was attracted to Zach. Very attracted.

"Hmm." Zach inhaled deeply. "There's nothing quite like the scent of frying burgers. Come, I promise you. A culinary delight awaits."

"How can a girl say no to that?"

She stood, but he didn't release his hold on her hand. His palm to hers felt hot as flame and far from comfortable. Not at all the way she expected. When Jay had held her hand, she'd felt...*lukewarm.*

Zach made her feel unsteady—how could that be? This was *Zach.* Her mechanic. Her friend. A fellow business owner.

"After you." He held the door for her.

When she slipped past him, the fine hair on her arms prickled.

He didn't appear to be affected by her as he ambled toward the red counter. A teenager approached and grabbed an order pad. Zach ordered, but his words sounded far away, and she couldn't make out what he was saying because her ears were ringing.

"Karen?" His hand lighted on her forearm, hot and scintillating, and the buzzing in her ears silenced. "What do you want? I recommend the cheeseburger. Nothing like it on this planet."

"That's an experience I'd better not miss."

"Good. I'm glad I'm with a woman who lives on the edge." He winked and ordered for her with the casual friendliness he'd always shown toward her.

When he withdrew his wallet from his back pocket, she stepped forward. "This is on Gramma."

"Forget it." Zach dropped a ten-dollar bill on the counter. "This is my treat. Your company is payment enough."

"My company?"

"Sure. I'm used to eating alone. Charm me with witty conversation and we'll call it even."

"You know I've never been witty in my entire life. I don't think it's a McKaslin family trait."

"Well, it only goes to show that you can't have everything. Status, beauty and brains will have to be enough."

"See what you're doing? One compliment after another. It's making me dizzy."

"Dizzy? I thought I was charming you."

"Nope. You're expelling too much hot air and contributing to the greenhouse effect."

He laughed, carrying a red plastic tray of food toward the condiment stand. He grabbed packets of ketchup and mustard. "Where do you want to sit?"

"In the corner, right in front of the air conditioner." She led the way, her skirt snapping above her knees and drawing his gaze.

Careful, Zach. It was hard to forget the way Karen's mom had glared at him as if she knew very well what he'd been thinking. And what he wanted when he looked at Karen.

He'd been foolish to hope for more than friendship. With or without another man's ring on her finger,

Karen would never be interested in him, the Drake boy who'd gotten into trouble at twelve. Whose mother had spent her days and nights at the local bar, unable to hold a job or take care of her children.

His step faltered. What did he think he was doing? Following Karen McKaslin around and hoping she might suddenly look at him—really look at him—and see the man he'd become. Like that was going to happen.

She slid into the booth as graceful as always. "That's one thing Gramma's car doesn't have—an air conditioner. I'd vowed my very next car would have one. When I *could* afford a new car, that is."

"Just be glad Helen's car has a heater. That's a step up from that rusted-out heap in my lot."

"Speaking of my old car, what do you think I should do with it?"

Zach set the tray on the table and sat across from her. So, he was back to being her mechanic. If he needed any proof of how Karen saw him, this was it.

He tucked away the disappointment. Wanting her was a dream; he'd known it all along.

"Let's say I make you an offer on the car. I'll fix her and sell her to someone really desperate for a set of wheels."

"It's a deal." Karen grabbed an onion ring from the paper holder and bit into it. "Mmm. This is delicious. I'll never doubt you again."

"Glad to hear it. It's about time you acknowledge my wisdom."

"Yes, you have great onion ring knowledge."

"Face it, I'm gifted."

"You're certainly something. I'm not sure *gifted* is the word I'd use."

"Hey. Be kind to me. Beneath all this greatness hides a fragile ego."

Her laughter was a gentle trill that washed over him. Zach couldn't help the zing of satisfaction in his chest or the tug of attraction as she took a second bite of the golden ring. Her mouth was soft pink and bow shaped. A truly beautiful mouth.

He had no right noticing. No right wondering what her kiss would feel like.

"How did you find out about this place?" she asked, taking another onion ring.

"When my brother was an undergraduate, he had an apartment not far from here. I'd stop by now and then and take him out to eat. I had to save him from his own cooking as much as I could."

"More like you were helping him stretch his food budget. You can't fool me."

"I imagine it's tough being a student. He worked nearly full-time with a full class load. My sister's doing the same."

"That brings back memories. Allison and I shared an apartment when we went to Montana State. Money was tight and we scraped by on what we both made working on campus, but those were good times I'll always remember."

"I took a few years of night classes at MSU," he

said, slurping on his strawberry milkshake. "I took courses for the small-business owner from the extended learning center. They helped me figure out how to do my own books. I liked it so well, I made sure my brother and sister could get their four-year degrees."

Karen heard what Zach didn't say. How he'd struggled through high school as the sole support of his younger siblings, and that couldn't have been easy. She realized that he helped them still, giving his brother and sister advantages he hadn't taken for himself.

She saw a new side to Zach and it left her speechless. His wide shoulders really did look like they could carry a family's burdens. Beneath his teasing humor was a strong and responsible man. Respect for him glowed like a warm ember in her chest, steady and strong, and lingered long after the meal ended.

The sun shot fire across the jagged peaks of the Rockies rimming the horizon, and the clouds burned with crimson and purple. Zach figured it was one of the best afternoons he'd had, spent with Karen.

He'd been stealing looks at her out of the corner of his eye as she drove down the highway. Maybe that's why he didn't notice there was something wrong with the car.

He leaned out the window, hoping to get a better look. It was a bad feeling as much as it was a mechanic's skill that told him the tiny plume of steam rising from beneath the polished hood was a sign of doom.

"Karen? Take a look at your gauges for me."

"Why? Think I'm speeding?" she asked as they left the highway behind, driving through golden fields toward town. "Ha! I never speed."

"I wasn't worried about the speedometer—"

"Heavens!" She gasped. "The temperature needle is on 'H'. Oh, and now there's a little bit of smoke coming from the hood. I'll pull over."

"Good idea." He waited while she stopped the car on the shoulder of the two-lane road. He hopped out onto the sun-baked pavement as soon as they stopped moving.

Not good. Steam hissed with wild venom as he unlatched the hood.

"An expert mechanic, huh?" Karen padded into sight around the front fender. "Guaranteed not to break down. Isn't that what you said?"

"Yep. That's what I said."

"Hmm." She sidled up to him and stared down at the radiator cap. "I'm no expert, but that looks like a problem to me."

"It sure does. We'll have to hike it the rest of the way to town."

"Good thing we don't have far to go, because I'm going to look up the mechanic who works on this car. I intend to give him a piece of my mind."

"That mechanic of yours is obviously not at fault." He joined her on the road. "Even a meticulously maintained car can suddenly crack a radiator. Come to think of it, it was probably the driver's fault.''

"My fault? I was driving the posted speed limit.''

"See what I mean? You bored the car to death. It decided to spring a leak just for a little excitement.''

"You're a bad man, blaming this all on me.''

"Then let's blame your grandmother. She's been driving that car for the last forty years. She must have known what condition it was in. She gave you a lemon.''

"Stop it. I'm laughing too hard to walk.''

"We can take a break. Sit down here next to the thistles and you can catch your breath.'' He gestured at the nuisance weeds at the side of the road. "Face it, I know how to show a lady a good time.''

"Well, I *have* been laughing a lot.'' How could that be? All her problems felt as if they'd floated away like dandelion fluff on the wind. There was no pressure on her chest, no worries weighing her down.

"Look.'' He gestured down the block where a gleaming red car was parked beneath the diner's striped awning. "Helen's already showing off her convertible. I hope she's having a good time.''

"Me, too.'' Karen recalled what her grandmother had said about how she wanted to be remembered. "I hope she's truly happy. Life is too precious to live the way everyone expects.''

"Newfound wisdom after sending Jay packing?''

"Something like that.'' She stopped in the shade

of the awning. "I can hitch a ride with Gramma or give one of my sisters a call."

"Then I guess it's goodbye."

He hated to admit it, but he couldn't keep Karen to himself any longer. One of her sisters, Kendra, was pushing through the screen door of the diner, calling out to her in excitement over the new convertible.

He backed away as she waved to him, the wind tangling sassy blond locks around her face, framing her beautiful face that made a man wish.

And keep wishing.

"What's with you and Zach?" Michelle asked as she pulled Karen by the arm into the diner. "You're with him in the morning, you go to church with him. And now it's nearly nighttime and where do I find you? Taking a walk with Mr. Tall, Dark and Handsome."

"Why are you looking at me like that? You know he only went to help Gramma negotiate a good price on her new car." Karen wasn't about to let Michelle know what a good time they'd had. "Zach and I were walking because the car broke down."

"No way. Zach's a great mechanic, and Gramma's car doesn't break down. Not in the history of the world as we know it. I think there's more to this." Michelle quirked one brow.

The last thing Karen wanted to talk about was Zachary Drake and her feelings for him—feelings that had become very confusing.

She spotted her grandmother in a nearby booth and walked over to her, figuring now was a good time to change the subject. "Gramma, how was the ride home?"

"Perfectly exciting. Why, I can't say the last time I had such a thrill. With the wind whistling in my ears and the world whizzing by at seventy miles an hour. I have to confess I had a hard time keeping to the speed limit."

"You lawbreaker." Karen knelt in the aisle next to the booth and said hello to her grandmother's friends. "Your eyes are sparkling. I'm glad you had a good time."

"And I'm taking Nora home in a bit. As soon as we finish our iced tea. And my dear Karen is following in my footsteps. Look how beautiful she is as a blonde. And only happiness can put that color in a girl's cheeks. Did you have a good time with Zach?"

Karen decided not to tell her grandmother about the damaged radiator. "I had a very good evening."

"Perfect. The new car was only one step of many I've been needing to take. Karen, I see a shopping trip in our future."

"Shopping for what?"

"Don't seem so surprised. My makeover isn't nearly complete and neither is yours, although you're making good progress." Trouble sparkled in Gramma's eyes. "Michelle, I see you and Kirby are enjoying ice cream on a Sunday night."

"Yeah, Gramma. You know us McKaslins, wild

girls to the core. C'mon, Karen, my sundae is melting.''

"Thanks for the car, Gramma." Karen pressed a kiss to her grandmother's cheek and stood. "You keep out of trouble."

Gramma laughed, and it felt good to see her looking happy.

Michelle leaned close as they made their way down the aisle. "Confess. Is Zach the real reason you broke up with Jay?"

"Yeah, tell us, Karen," her sister Kirby asked from the nearby booth. "Is he the reason you colored your hair? Everyone is talking about it. Going to church with him and not with Jay. Did you really think anyone *wouldn't* notice?"

"There's nothing to notice," she alibied. "Now move over. That sundae looks pretty good."

Michelle grabbed a spoon from the counter and dropped it on the table. "Okay, now we're together, out with it. We want to know what's really going on."

"The truth is that you're just nosy."

"We're your sisters. We have the right."

"Yeah, we have to know which rumors to believe and which to ignore." Kirby nudged the ice cream dish closer so they could share. "Without a doubt, Zach's the most handsome man in this county. Are you going after him?"

"What? It's nothing like that. He's just..." Heat warmed her face and she couldn't deny the attraction she felt. Thinking of him made her pulse race. "He's a *friend*."

"And getting closer by the minute." Michelle waggled her brows.

"Don't tease her like that," Kirby admonished, waving her ice cream spoon in the air. "We don't want her to get stubborn and refuse to cooperate. C'mon, Karen. Tell the truth. You two look pretty cozy. He comes by your shop every morning."

"He's a customer, really."

"You're over at his garage quite a bit," Michelle accused. "Oh, and he likes to drive you home."

"When my car dies and leaves me stranded."

"Your car is dying quite a bit lately."

"But it's the truth!" Karen exclaimed.

Her sisters laughed too hard to be able to eat.

So did she. "All right, I give up. I admit it. Zachary Drake is the best-looking man in the entire state of Montana. Are you happy now?"

"I am," Zach answered as he laid the car key on the worn Formica table.

"Zach?" Karen saw his sneakers stop in the aisle next to her table. She didn't dare look up. He'd heard her say—

"I put some stuff in the radiator to seal the crack and parked it out front, but you'll need to bring it in one day so I can fix the problem."

"Great. Thanks." Karen choked on the words as she stared at the fascinating tabletop. Beside her, her sister was shaking with the effort to hold back laughter. "I'll give you a call."

"I'll be looking forward to it. Oh, and Karen, I think you're pretty good-looking, too."

Her sisters burst into howls as Zach walked away. She couldn't get mad at them, because she'd embarrassed herself. "Stop that. Michelle, you had to be able to see him, so you knew he was coming to our table."

"Guilty as charged, but how was I to know what you were going to say? I think he likes you, sis."

Both Kirby and Michelle nodded vigorously.

"I know what you guys are thinking, but I'm *not* looking for a replacement for Jay." Karen grabbed her spoon and dug into the chocolate-sauce-covered ice cream. "My heart has taken enough blows."

"Then Zach can be your rebound romance," Kirby offered sensibly, stealing the cherry from the top of the sundae.

"Yeah, he can help you get over Jay." Michelle seemed pleased with herself as she gestured toward the windows. "Look at him all alone, a man as gorgeous as that."

"He *is* gorgeous," Kirby agreed.

"I know." Karen stared through the dusty window, her heart tugging painfully at the sight of the man ambling across the street. "We're friends, that's all. We have a good time together."

"Still holding on to regrets with Jay?" Kirby asked.

"No regrets." Karen licked the chocolate topping off her spoon, holding back the truth. There were some things she couldn't tell anyone. She was plain and ordinary. She'd never done anything daring or exciting in her entire life, and she was tired of it.

Lukewarm. That's what Gramma had called it.

Karen couldn't give voice to the fear that she would always be seen as sensible, dependable Karen when her heart craved so much more.

"Look, it's Mr. Winkler." Michelle gulped down a mouthful of ice cream. "He's walking over to Gramma. Think he's impressed by her new car?"

Karen scrambled in the cramped booth for a view around the back of the tall seat.

Beside her, Kirby did the same. "Ooh, they're talking. I can almost hear them."

There was no way Mr. Winkler would see Gramma as lukewarm now. She looked so happy, glowing with life and beauty. She was going to charm the socks off of the poor man. Triumph jolted through Karen's chest as she watched Clyde Winkler greet Gramma with a polite nod.

"Nice to see you girls here," Clyde was saying, his low baritone was friendly. "Helen, why'd you go and change your hair like that for?"

"Why, because I felt like it, Clyde. Enjoy your evening." Gramma twisted away from him and she took a long drink from her iced tea, turning her back to the man in the aisle, who gave a shrug and walked away.

"Poor Gramma." Karen knew her grandmother had to be hurting.

"Way harsh." Michelle shook her head in apparent disbelief. "I mean, he didn't even compliment her. Dawn did such a fabulous job with her hair."

"Maybe it isn't about the hair," Kirby argued. "Gramma's looked practically the same since I can remember. People get comfortable with who you are and expect to always see you that way."

Like reliable. Dependable. Karen peered around the booth to where her grandmother sat, nursing her iced tea and what had to be a wounded heart.

There was no doubt about it. Sometimes a woman wanted more.

Chapter Six

The rattle on the back door echoed through the morning-bright shop. Karen nearly dropped the nearly full frothing pitcher. She eased to the end of the counter and strained to look around the wall.

It's him.

On the other side of the glass door, Zach waved, looking twice as handsome as he'd been the last time she saw him, even in his plain T-shirt and jeans.

Be calm, she coached herself as she snapped the to-go lid on the cup of steaming coffee. Just pretend he didn't hear what you said about him last night. He knows we're just friends, right?

Her face felt a shade hotter as she hurried to the glass door, his gaze as bold as a touch. He leaned against the door frame, with the golden sunlight kissing his dark locks. Had a man ever looked this good?

As if he were perfectly aware of the impression he

made, he shaded his eyes with one hand and winked when he spotted her. His eyes sparkled as if he was very glad to see her.

He apparently hadn't forgotten what she'd said—sure, it had been just last night, but was it too much to hope for momentary amnesia?

A strange sense of panic ripped through her, leaving her weak as she tugged open the door. Sweet hot wind breezed between them and, like a hug, pulled her close to him.

"Hey, you were expecting me." He gestured at the cup she held. "Either that, or you're hoping to get rid of me real quick."

"What? Get rid of my favorite customer?" She pushed the cup into his hands and tried to look innocent.

"Your favorite customer, huh? I like the sound of that."

"I meant my *best* customer."

"Sure you did. It's too late, and you can't fool me anymore." Trouble flashed in his eyes. "Mind if I come in? This'll only take a minute."

"I've got my bread delivery to sort—"

"You don't need bread until lunchtime. This can't wait." He pulled an envelope from his back pocket. "Payment for your old car. Got the title?"

"Not with me."

"You look like a trustworthy girl. You can get it to me later." He tossed the envelope onto the nearby table. "There's my best offer. Take it or leave it, although it's a darn good deal."

"I'm afraid to guess. If that old rust heap is worth twenty bucks, I'll be shocked."

"Twenty bucks? I should have negotiated. I bet I could've got the car for a steal. But no, I wanted to be fair." He winked at her.

He was far too sure of himself. And she knew why. "You do know the danger in overhearing other people's conversations, don't you?"

"Climbing cliffs, skydiving—now that's dangerous. But eavesdropping? Last night I was just an innocent guy walking through the café when I happened to hear what you were saying about me. A man's interest perks up when he hears a woman mention his name."

"That's the danger. You didn't listen to the *entire* conversation. My sisters were talking about how homely they thought you were, and I was trying to defend your honor."

"My honor needs defending?"

"Something like that. I was commenting on your looks in the most objective of terms."

"I see." He winked, as if he knew exactly what she was trying to do. As if he could see straight through her teasing to the truth beneath. "It's not like you think I'm handsome."

"Exactly."

"I don't think you're pretty, either." He struggled not to laugh.

This wasn't funny at all. Her attempt to set things right had backfired.

She grabbed the envelope and thumbed through the crisp bills inside. ''There's more than a few hundred dollars in here.''

''Blue book value.''

''No way. This is too much money for an old car that doesn't run.''

''A lie for a lie, gorgeous.'' He pressed a kiss to her cheek, a soft brush of heat across her skin.

Time froze and in the space between one breath and the next, Karen felt the tension knotted in her muscles melt away, leaving her warm and weak.

And aware. Much too aware. He smelled like late-summer sunshine, fresh air and Old Spice, and the day's growth on his jaw scraped against her skin. Every nerve ending felt enlivened.

Through the buzzing in her ears, Karen heard the distant ring of the phone and sound of footsteps as Zach moved away. The sweetness of his kiss remained as she stumbled to the counter and nearly dropped the receiver.

''Field of Beans Coffee Shop, how can I help you?'' she said automatically into the mouthpiece, but the familiar words felt awkward on her tongue. Her entire being tingled.

''Karen, is Zach there?'' The gravelly baritone of the local fire chief's voice boomed cross the line. ''We've got a lost hiker and we need him.''

Zach? ''How did you know he was here?''

"I've got eyes just like everyone else in town. Tell him to grab his coffee and get his behind over here pronto." The line clicked.

Karen set her handheld phone on the counter.

Zach lifted one dark brow. "That was for me?"

"The fire chief says he needs you." Karen rubbed her forehead because a pain began jackknifing through her skull. "He knew you were here."

"I'm here every morning just about, rain or shine." Zach leaned across the counter and cupped her chin with his hand. His skin was rough and callused but felt more comforting than any touch she'd ever known.

"When Search and Rescue calls, I've got to go." Then he released her, ambling toward the door. "I'll be seeing you, gorgeous. You keep on thinking about how handsome you find me."

"I lied about that."

"You're too nice to do something awful like lie."

"Nice. Is that what you think of me?" It felt like a blow, maybe because that's how Jay had always complimented her. She tucked her disappointment deep inside so it wouldn't show. "Then maybe I'd better tell you the truth I've been hiding all along. You're a homely man, Zachary Drake."

A dimple cut into his cheek when he grinned. "That's not what you told your sisters. I'll see you tomorrow, so be prepared."

"That sounds like a warning. Or maybe a threat."

"Both." He tipped his Stetson and strode through the doors and out of sight.

Leaving behind the scent of Old Spice and the rapid beat of her heart.

I'm not falling for him, she vowed. Absolutely, positively not.

But the memory of Zach's kiss remained.

She let me kiss her. He still couldn't believe it. It was like something from a dream that could never be real. But it *was.*

Her cheek had felt as soft as new silk, and he'd inhaled the scent of her shampoo. Faint vanilla clung to him, proof of what had happened between them.

Nope, he still couldn't believe it. He'd kissed her, and she hadn't pulled away in shock. Hadn't slapped him, called him names or run for the hills.

In fact, she must have liked it. She had this little dazed look on her face, and then a small smile teased at the corner of her soft bow-shaped lips.

Watch it, Zach. He'd only get into trouble if he started thinking about her mouth, because he'd want to try kissing her there next.

He felt a slap on his shoulder, jostling him out of his thoughts.

"Zach, grab your climbing gear. We're here."

"Sure thing, Chief." He grabbed his backpack and hopped over the bed of the four-wheel drive. His feet hit the ground, reminding him of the missing hiker and the team of searchers needing his cooperation.

He had to concentrate and focus, but with the way Karen's vanilla scent clung to his skin, he couldn't forget her. Or how she tried to hide her true feelings this morning.

Karen McKaslin liked him—*really* liked him. Impossible, but true.

He grabbed his water canteen and jogged to catch up with the men.

"Something wrong?"

Karen jumped, and the money she held flew across the table. "Gramma. I didn't hear you."

"Left your back door unlocked." Her grandmother's step echoed in the empty coffee shop. "Saw the car in the lot and thought I'd come in and check on you, and I'm glad I did. You look tired."

"I had a busy day."

"It's more than that." Gramma pulled out a chair, settling down with a sigh. "That looks like a good day's earnings."

"It's from Zach. He bought my old car and paid way too much for it." Karen gathered up the crisp bills and folded them in half. She hadn't decided what she was going to do about his generosity, just as she hadn't figured out what to do about his kiss.

And that kiss was something Gramma wasn't going to know about, no matter how much she pried. "Did you race around in your new convertible today?"

"You're changing the subject, and because I tend to be nosy, I have to wonder why."

"Keep wondering, because I'm not telling you." Karen slipped Zach's money into her shirt pocket. "How's your makeover coming along?"

"There's still room for improvement. I can't keep raiding relative's closets forever. Mine is full of dresses I never really liked, but I bought them because they were sensible and on sale."

"When you wanted something else," Karen guessed. She knew what that was like. Hadn't she purchased her own shapeless purple T-shirt and denim shorts on sale two years ago?

"What I need is a good old-fashioned shopping spree. I heard an advertisement on my fancy new car radio, so I know the mall in Bozeman is having a back-to-school sale. I bet I can find a whole new wardrobe in a place like that."

"The chances are good, but you should take Michelle with you. She's the fashion guru of the family. I don't think the rest of us have ever opened a fashion magazine."

"I have a different assignment for Michelle, so don't you worry about her. And besides, my dear, there is nothing wrong with your fashion sense. I do have the best-looking granddaughters in the county, hands down. Everyone at the Ladies' Aid agrees."

"You aren't going to mention marriage and grand-babies again, are you?"

"Heavens, no! That will come in time, I have no doubt about it."

"Probably not for me." Karen stared through the

windows at the quiet, dusty street spread out before her.

She'd grown up in this tiny town, and not one thing she'd ever imagined for her life had come true. She'd always figured she'd be married by now, keeping house, raising children and being a wife. She'd always pictured her husband to be kind. Someone who made her laugh. Someone who returned her love.

Maybe all it had ever been was a dream.

Remembering how Clyde had treated Gramma at the diner and of Gramma's confession about her marriage made Karen sad. Was romantic love a fantasy and nothing more?

Or, maybe, true love didn't happen to women like her.

Karen knew she wasn't particularly pretty or exciting. If she needed proof of that, she had it—she'd won the citizenship award in school every year since the sixth grade. And now, over ten years later, she was still a play-by-the-rules kind of girl who could never inspire a deep, powerful love in a man.

That's what she wanted—a true, abiding love. Not a comfortable sort of marriage without warmth or passion, but the kind of relationship that dreams were made of. And her heart desired.

Gramma's hands covered hers, warm and comforting. "Why does my granddaughter look so troubled?"

"When Zach was over this morning for his cup of

coffee, he said I was a 'nice' girl. But I know what he meant—reliable. Dependable. *Lukewarm.*''

"It's hard for stellar women like us to be labeled that way. That's why I'm making over my life. We're stuck in a rut, you and me."

"A big long rut I'll never get out of. It's not like I want to take up bad habits and break laws."

"I know. You just want to find your heart. So do I. That's why I think you and I ought to have a little fun at the mall. We'll shop until we drop, just like the advertisement promised."

"I'd love to, but I can't spare the funds right now. And, no—you're not buying me anything. You've done too much for me as it is. Besides, I can't afford to take any time off. It affects sales and I've got that big nasty balloon payment coming up."

"That's right. I've been thinking about that, too."

"*No.* You're not helping me, so forget it. This is my business and my problem. Keep your money in your checkbook where it belongs."

Gramma turned thoughtful. "Running a business by yourself isn't easy. In the beginning, you had Allison to take over and give you a break, as you could do for her. Now you're alone without backup. I have the perfect solution. Do you know what you need? Hired help."

"I'm doing fine on my own."

Trouble flickered in Gramma's eyes, as if she'd planned this all along. "Your littlest sister could use a second job. Michelle's position over at the Snip &

Style is on appointment only, and isn't full-time yet. Considering how she's been a tad irresponsible with her credit cards, she could use some extra income.''

"I'd love to pay her, but I can't dip into my savings to do it.''

"Why don't you offer her the job, and maybe things will work out? The Good Lord provides, you know, and He does command us to honor our elders. As I see it, that means you have to come shopping with me.''

"You do? That's manipulative and you know it.''

"Yes, but you did promise to help me, and there's a coffee shop in the mall. We could stop by and see what the competition is up to.''

"I like the way you think, Gramma.''

"Then that's one thing settled. You still haven't told me about you and Zachary Drake.''

"We're just friends and you know it.'' Or was he? A *friend* didn't make a woman's pulse race or cause her to think about him when he wasn't in the room.

"Zach's easy on the eyes, I'll grant you that.'' Gramma winked. "He was such a help with my car purchase. Getting the price so low, I don't know how he did it! Why, he's a gem, and I need to find a way to repay him.''

"I'm sure he isn't expecting anything.''

"A thank-you gesture is always in good style, expected or not. You know him better than I do. What does he like?''

"I don't know him that well. He fishes. He rides

his motorcycle. He likes bologna on white with mustard.''

"He's a bachelor. There has to be something I can do for him."

"You could cook for him." The idea came to her like a whisper on the wind. "The night my old car died, he was chiseling frozen hot dogs out of his freezer when I called. So I fed him our supper leftovers, and he confessed he eats frozen dinners."

"Those things from the grocery store? You mean to tell me the poor man can't cook at all?"

"I owe him a big favor, too, so maybe the two of us could spend time in the kitchen and make him a bunch of homemade frozen dinners."

"Perfect." Gramma clapped her hands together. "Oh, he did seem to love my taco cheese and macaroni casserole. Let's do it the first chance we get. That's something he might appreciate."

"You're on. Right now I've got to make the deposit. Want to go with me?"

"We'll take my car." Gramma stole the bank bag from the counter and headed for the door.

That was one problem solved. Karen grabbed her keys. As her fingers closed around the cool metal, she realized this was the exact spot she'd been standing in when he'd kissed her this morning.

It's not like it was a real kiss. Just a brush of his lips to her cheek. A friendly gesture, that was all.

So why had she thought about it through every moment of the day? Or remembered how solid and masculine he'd seemed when he'd stood so close to her?

I'm not falling for him, she ordered herself. She'd never love another man—no matter how good—who wanted nice and dependable.

"You did a fine job today, Zach." Chief Corey halted his truck in the middle of town. "We're lucky to have a climber as skilled as you on our team."

"You were the one who gave the young man medical treatment, not me." Zach grabbed his gear from the pickup's bed. "Bring this piece of junk by sometime tomorrow and I'll fix that misfire. Sounds terrible."

"Yeah, but it makes all the pretty women look at me."

"With disgust."

"We can't all be as lucky as you, dating Karen McKaslin. She looks downright beautiful with her new hairdo."

"John, I don't think you ought to be noticing Karen's beauty. You just leave that to me. I'll do a good job of it."

The chief pulled away, chuckling. Zach slung his pack over his shoulder and headed up the sidewalk. Exhaustion hung on him like a hundred-pound weight, and the sun's heat baking him clear through to the bones didn't help much.

What he needed was a root beer. Frothy and fizzing and so icy it would make a cold trail down his throat.

Too bad he didn't have one in his empty refrigerator.

Zach tossed his pack on the ground and fished through a zippered compartment for his shop keys. Maybe he'd run down to the grocery and pick up a six-pack of root beer and maybe a frozen pizza. He might as well splurge after spending most of the day hiking in ninety-degree temperatures and half the afternoon scaling a tricky canyon wall.

A horn blared. He looked up to see a sporty red convertible with tiny Helen behind the wheel and Karen in the passenger seat.

At the sight of her, he forgot every discomfort. Her golden locks were tangled from the drive with the top down and framed her heart-shaped face. The grape shirt she wore clung to her softly, emphasizing her small frame. The color made her eyes so blue that her beauty astounded him.

How was it that she became more stunning every time he looked at her?

"Howdy, gorgeous." He left his gear on the concrete and ambled over to the street. "I can't believe my eyes. Two lovely women parked in front of my shop. It's good for business."

"You're filthy." Karen shook her head at him in mock disapproval. "Looks like you've been up to no good."

"Like always."

"I heard at the bank that you played hero and rescued a poor stranded tourist who found himself stuck on a cliff.''

"He learned scaling a canyon wall is harder than it looks, even if you can afford the equipment. His wife's indebted to me for saving her husband's life and completely adores me. At least *she* has good judgment.''

That made Karen laugh. She lit up like a Montana sunset—all quiet beauty that a man never got tired of looking at.

"Get out if you two are going to talk,'' Helen complained, glancing at the rearview mirror. "I don't want to create a traffic jam because you two are carrying on a love affair right here in the middle of the street.''

"We're not carrying on, Gramma.''

"Yes, we are.'' Zach opened the passenger door and held it.

Karen frowned at him as if she were angry, but she couldn't fool him—her eyes were sparkling. Was she remembering that kiss he'd dared to give her? He hadn't been able to think of much else all day.

"See you two kids later.'' Helen waved as she drove off.

He was alone with Karen. Just the two of them.

Now this was a nice turn of events.

"I've got something for you.'' Karen reached into her back pocket and withdrew a folded document. "The promised title, signed and everything.''

"You were trustworthy after all.''

"You say that as if you worried."

"It was a gamble." He could stand here looking at Karen all evening, but he took the title she offered him and led the way up the driveway. "That's the only reason you came over. To give me the title?"

"I really want to argue with you about the money you paid me."

"It's my policy never to renegotiate a price after a deal's been made."

"How did I know you were going to say that?"

"Argue all you want. It won't do a bit of good." He grabbed his keys and slung his pack over his shoulder. "Want to come up? But I have to warn you the air-conditioning only works when it feels like it."

"Can't you fix it?"

"That would be too easy." He led the way up the stairs at the side of the garage. "Have any more trouble with that radiator?"

"No. I noticed you didn't bill me for delivering it to me at the café."

"You didn't charge me for my coffee this morning. We're even, so forget it." He unlocked the door and reached inside to flick on the light. "It's humble, but it's home."

She brushed past him, all sweetness and woman. "I'm speechless. Do you ever dust?"

"Me? Dust? It's a waste of time. It just falls right back on the TV anyway." He tried the air-conditioning and the unit surprised him by coughing to life.

"You don't cook. You don't dust." Karen shook her head as she paced the length of his small living room. She stopped by the desk in the corner where his computer sat dark and silent. She ran her fingertips over the frames on the wall above it. "Special awards from the governor for your work on Search and Rescue. How come I didn't know about these?"

"You've never been in my apartment before, and I'm too modest to brag."

"You saved people's lives before this, just like you did today."

"The hiker overestimated his abilities, that's all. And besides, I don't work alone. I'm only part of a team."

She frowned as if she didn't believe him, but at least she changed the subject. "This is something I should do. There's attic space above my shop. Maybe I could convert it into an apartment."

"You live with your parents?"

"Not in their house. In the apartment over the garage. It isn't much. Dad always rented it to his foreman, but he hires seasonally now. I talked them into staying there when my mother became ill. It was easier than driving to and from town at night."

"Your family means a lot to you." Zach flicked on the air-conditioning unit in the kitchen window. "How's your mom doing?"

"A little better, although she's pretty unhappy there isn't going to be a wedding. I've disappointed her, she says. I know she was counting on it to lift her spirits.''

"So, find another brilliant, handsome and irresistible man and marry him instead.'' Or me, he added silently. He snared two cups from the shelf and filled them with tap water.

He dropped ice cube chunks iced together into the cups. It was the best he could do under the circumstances. And it was a shame, too, because this was not going to impress her.

"Getting married is the last thing I want to do.''

"You don't want to get married? I thought that's what all women wanted.'' Zach said it casually, crossing the room to hand her a drink.

"Water in a cartoon cup?''

"That's class. You don't get this kind of service just anywhere.'' Zach shoved grease-smeared truck magazines off the coffee table. "You never told me why you're running around single.''

"No, and I don't plan to.''

"It's top secret. Is that it?''

"Highly confidential. I could be hauled before a grand jury if I revealed what I know.'' Karen sipped the water, leaning back on the couch. She was long and lean and looked mighty pretty in his living room. "Do you ever get tired of living alone?''

"Yeah, and every single woman who comes along starts looking mighty attractive. It's tempting to give up my wild ways and settle down, but then how could I move out of this place?''

"You can't fool me. It gets lonely being single."

"It does."

She stared into her cup, unhappiness apparent on her face. "I just don't want to settle."

"Neither do I."

Now he knew what was wrong and what she wanted. He didn't know all that had made her gun-shy about marriage, and maybe it wasn't his business, but he could see how vulnerable she seemed, small on his big bulky secondhand couch.

And so fine. Like rare porcelain, so dainty and fragile. And probably far out of his class—there was no doubt about that. But at least now he had a chance. She liked him, he could tell by the way she smiled.

"What am I going to do with you?" she asked. "We really need to talk about what happened this morning."

"When I ran out without paying for my coffee?"

"That's not what I mean and you know it." A blush stole across her face. "You kissed me."

"No, I thought you kissed *me*."

"Zach!" He was incorrigible, teasing her! "Don't get me wrong. It was very nice, but—"

"You're afraid I'm too handsome for you to resist?"

"I'm not the one who has problems with restraint. You kissed me, remember?"

"Think I might do it again? Or are you afraid you might want me to?"

"You are a bad man. You know that's not what I

mean.'' She set down her cup and stood, marching to the door. ''I just want to check and make sure. That was just a *friendly* kiss you gave me, right?''

''Absolutely. That was a one-hundred-percent-friend kiss.''

He opened the door for her, so close she could see the rise and fall of his wide chest as he breathed. ''We're friends, just like you say.''

''Good.'' At least that was settled.

She stepped into the sunshine and heat, feeling a strange disappointment at leaving him. It was a feeling she couldn't explain.

She didn't want more than friendship. She'd just failed at a romance. The last thing she needed was to fail again because the man she liked thought she was a certain type of person.

''There's just one more thing.'' She forced her gaze to his. ''I'm not nice. Don't ever insult me by saying that again.''

He grinned slow and saucy. ''I'll try to remember that, you wild, untamed woman.''

''That's more like it. I live on the edge and don't you forget it.''

''I'll try, *friend*.''

She didn't know why the sound of his laughter warmed her clear through to her soul, like comfort and peace and coming home.

Friends. That's what they were, and getting closer with every day.

She took the steps two at a time, wondering if that's what the Lord was trying to tell her. That it was time to make some changes, have a little fun and enjoy this life she'd been given.

Chapter Seven

"I can handle making iced lattes for a few hours, so chill." Michelle looked in command behind the counter that Karen had just finished cleaning. "I've done this before."

"Yeah, but now I'm paying you, so be good, little sister." Karen grabbed her keys, slung her purse strap over her shoulder and headed out the back door.

Freedom. The sun felt sweeter, the breeze gentler as she sauntered along the wooden walk. Her baskets of sweet peas waved as she passed, their scent as welcome as this stolen time.

Gramma was right. Taking some time to herself was a great idea. She felt lighter, freer, as she approached her reliable car, gleaming in the sunshine.

The engine started with a single turn of the key. She loved having a dependable vehicle—except for the small crack in the radiator, which wasn't causing any problems. With the windows rolled down, she cranked up the Christian music station and let the wind blow through her hair as she drove.

She couldn't help noticing that the wide doors to Zach's garage were locked up tight. The memory of his kiss brushed across her cheek, and she felt... No! She wasn't going to feel anything. That was a friendly kiss, and he'd gone to the trouble to assure her of it. He wouldn't mislead her, would he?

Of course not. He'd stood with all the integrity in the world and told her he saw her as a friend. Without blinking or flinching.

So what was the problem? *She* was beginning to feel something more than friendship toward him.

That was definitely the problem.

Troubled, she sang along with the radio as she drove home. The harvested fields stretched out on either side of the road, golden brown and endless. She saw a tall column of dust on the crest of a nearby rolling hill and spotted Dad's tractor, turning soil. She honked and saw him wave his hat in return.

By the time she'd pulled into the shade of the garage, she wasn't feeling calm at all. Muscles knotted along the back of her neck and deep in her shoulders. She might as well have stayed at work!

Just stop thinking about Zach. That was all.

Resolved, she climbed the stairs to her cozy apartment over the garage. When she opened the door, sweltering heat met her and she opened the windows wide. What she needed was an air-conditioning unit, like the ones Zach had.

Okay, she *couldn't* stop thinking about him. What she needed to do was to distract herself completely. Forget Zachary Drake. But how?

In her bedroom, she changed into a pair of jeans and pulled on her riding boots. After tying her hair back, she found her Stetson. On the way out the door, she grabbed a handful of peppermint candies and stuffed them into her front pockets.

I wonder where Zach is? she thought, then shook her head. Enough, already. This was her afternoon off and she was going to enjoy it.

She strolled down the path from the garage to the stable without thinking of Zach. See, it was possible. Surely she could get through the rest of the day without thinking of him.

Star nickered in greeting, trotting up to the rail fence, her coat gleaming like polished copper. Her platinum mane caught the wind as she sidestepped, eager for company.

"Hey, girl." Karen grabbed the bridle from the rung just inside the stable door, then climbed through the fence. "How about a wild ride, just the two of us?"

Star swung her head, as if in agreement, and tugged at Karen's clothes.

"Found the peppermint, did you?" She unwrapped two candies and laid one on her palm. Star lipped up the mint.

Karen popped the other in her mouth. It took only a minute to secure the bridle and hop onto Star's back. She gathered the reins and urged the horse into an easy lope through the golden fields.

Larks argued in the cottonwoods as Karen and Star headed for the river. There was nothing like this—just her and her horse, the friendly companionship, the rock of Star's gait and the heat of her coat.

Karen felt the tension melt away from her neck and shoulders. Soon the river came into view and the sight took her breath away. Sunlight sparkled in the lazy waters, and a frog leaped from the shore and out of sight.

Star tugged at the bit, eager to be off, and as she always did, Karen gave the mare her head. The horse leaped into a smooth gallop, stretching full out on the public trail that paralleled the river. There was no one around, so Karen leaned low over Star's neck, urging her faster.

It was like flying without sound, rising and falling, and feeling the strength and life of the animal beneath her. She was right—this was just the thing to forget all her troubles. See how she wasn't thinking of Zach?

There she was, doing it again. Okay, so he was handsome, kind, funny, generous and he made her *feel.* That didn't mean it was a good idea—

She saw a blur of movement careen around a corner in the trail and Star sidestepped, whinnying in fear. The blur became a flashy mountain bike and rider moving fast. She felt the mare tense as if readying to rear, but she was off balance and started to slip.

"Whoa, girl," she soothed, tightening the reins, hoping to draw the mare's head down.

Star's nose dropped to the ground, and Karen kept her seat.

"Hey, sorry about that. I didn't mean to startle your horse." The rider skidded to a stop. Brakes squealed and dust plumed in the air.

Up Star went into a full rear, pawing the air with a panicked neigh. In the back of Karen's mind, she recognized that man's voice, but her legs were sliding out from under her. The ground looked pretty hard. Falling off wouldn't be the best experience.

Clamping her thighs harder around the mare's sides didn't stop Karen from slipping. Her hat tumbled off her head, so she dismounted swiftly, shortening the reins as she went.

Star dropped to the ground, still frightened.

Soothing the mare with her voice, Karen ran her hand up the horse's neck, calming her. "I hope you're happy, you irresponsible—"

"Karen, are you okay?" Zach dropped his bike and raced to her side.

Star sidestepped, whinnying in protest.

"Zach? What were you doing speeding?"

"I wasn't speeding." He grabbed her by the arm. "When I saw your horse rear like that, I had visions of you falling and breaking your neck. Are you really all right?"

"No, I'm not all right." She jerked away from his touch. "You were going too fast and someone could have gotten hurt. What if it had been one of the little girls who ride their ponies on this trail? They might not have known how to handle a frightened pony and—"

"Karen." He cupped the side of her face with his hand. "I wasn't going that fast. I ride fast when I'm on the road, but not on a public trail. Your horse and I startled each other."

"But you just came around the corner so fast!"

"Maybe you weren't paying attention." He drew her into his arms. "Feel that. I was so scared for you, I'm still shaking."

"*You?* Scared?" she quipped. "I don't believe it, a tough guy like you."

"Not so tough. See?" He pulled her all the way against his chest.

Her spine stiffened. The last thing she wanted to be was this close to Zach. Safe and protected in his arms, with the side of her face pressed against his solid chest, she could hear his heartbeat thunder.

His hand curled around the back of her neck, under her hair, holding her tenderly. "I don't see why you want to ride something that can buck you off."

"I love my horse."

"I love my bike." His words vibrated through her, so intimately, it left her breathless.

She desperately searched for a quick comeback to make him laugh, to make them both laugh so she could step out of his arms and everything would be as it was. They would be friends, *just* friends.

She couldn't think of a single quip. Handsome, came to mind. Amazing and wonderful. But her heart broke a little, and she couldn't begin to tell him what she truly felt.

His hand cupping her jaw grew hotter, his touch more tender. This was Zach, she reminded herself. Her mechanic and friend. She'd known him since kindergarten.

Well, she hadn't really known him at all. Maybe she'd never looked hard enough or noticed the man he'd become.

She noticed now. His chest felt like sun-warmed steel beneath her palm. Her heart began to tumble as he leaned forward slowly, deliberately.

This was going to be a real kiss, lip to lip, the kind that could never be mistaken for a *friendly* kiss. The kind that would mean they were more than friends. The type of kiss a man gave a woman.

Zach's mouth hovered over hers, a brush of heat she wanted to welcome. But how could she? She wasn't ready, so she backed away from the warm haven of his arms.

A crooked smile curved across his lips, but it was the disappointment she saw in his gaze that troubled her. She'd hurt him when she hadn't meant to. She'd only been protecting her heart.

"I know my charm can be overwhelming," he

quipped as he rescued his fallen mountain bike. "You'll get used to it."

"You think you're charming, do you?" She grabbed Star's reins from the grass at the side of the trail, where the mare was grazing. "*Charming* isn't the word I'd use."

"Dashing? Captivating?"

"Now you're getting closer." She mounted her horse. "Too bad it's all in your imagination."

"Really? Then why'd you let me almost kiss you? You wanted it. I could tell."

"You have to practice on somebody. Since you seem deficient when it comes to certain social situations, I was only trying to help you out."

"That's downright neighborly of you, Karen."

"That's me. Neighborly to the core." She gazed down at him, the wind tangling the golden strands worked loose from her ponytail.

A pleasant pink flushed her cheeks, and even though she'd stepped away from him, she wasn't mad. The way Zach figured it, she'd wanted that kiss. Judging by the way that her eyes were sparkling, he'd have another chance.

She needed time, and he could give her that. He'd give her anything, truth be told, if only he could have the right one day to make her his.

Marriage was serious business and the thought of it shot a cold chill down his spine, but he wasn't afraid. Well, not *too* afraid.

He'd loved Karen most of his life. God willing, it would be an honor to love her for the rest of his days.

He spied her Stetson in the wild grasses and retrieved it. "Forget something?"

"Thanks."

She swiped it out of his grip so fast, she seemed nervous. Or unnerved. Good. Let her wonder what that kiss would have been like. Because he already knew. Kissing Karen would be like coming home. Like finding the missing piece of his heart.

He mounted his bike. "Where are you headed?"

"To town. Star and I used to always ride to get ice cream, but we haven't done it so much lately." Karen tipped her hat, trying to avoid his gaze.

"Don't tell me your horse eats ice cream."

"She loves butterscotch sundaes as much as I do."

Something changed in the way Karen looked at him, as if she were seeing the man he was and not just the friend he'd been. He liked that. "I have a soft spot for double chocolate fudge cones."

"I don't suppose a tough cyclist like you would want to come along with us."

"My bike scares your horse."

"Not if you ride *slowly*." She laid the reins against her mare's neck, turning the animal on the trail. "Is that a yes?"

"Just promise you won't fall off that animal and break your neck. Horses make me nervous."

"Oh, this from a man who rides a *motorcycle*."

Maybe it was the way she rolled her eyes or the drop of warmth in her voice, but his heart opened wide.

Dust rose on the late-afternoon breezes as they rode side by side through town. Karen noticed several people looking at them. A few cars and pickups passed by, waving a hello.

"You left Michelle alone in the coffee shop?" Zach asked, chuckling warm and deep. "You're joking, right?"

"No joke." Karen felt warm all over from listening to his laugh. He had such a *great* laugh. "I was feeling brave."

"The sister who turned your hair green."

"The very one. It was Gramma's idea, and I hate to admit it, but she's right. A few afternoons off a week is what I need."

"And you trust Michelle not to burn the place down while you're gone?"

"I know where she lives. Just in case."

A few shoppers peered through the glass front window of the combination gift and flower shop to stare at them. Every one of the customers wore a look of surprise *and* speculation.

Like it's their business, Karen told herself. The problem with a small town was that there wasn't enough traffic jams to distract people from noticing every little thing a person did.

Just because she was riding down the street with Zachary Drake *did not mean anything.*

Well, that wasn't true. They were friends. Good friends. Friends close enough to share a friendly kiss now and maybe more. She'd had fun this afternoon listening to him laugh. He had a great laugh. Oh, right, she'd already noticed that.

It wasn't like she was falling for him.

Please, Lord, don't let me fall for him.

"Wow. Busy place." Zach skidded his bike to a stop in the loose gravel. "Don't tell me you're going to ride up to the window. There are little kids waiting in line there. What about your horse?"

"Trust me. Star and I might be out of practice, but we've been coming here together since I was eight."

"I remember." Zach nodded toward a little girl and her pony getting an ice cream cone at the outside window of the little shop. "You and your sister were like that, always together and almost always with your horses."

"Like half the little girls in this town." Karen nosed Star toward the end of the line behind two boys with fancy bikes and money clutched in their fists.

"Hi, Zach," Tommy Clemmins, one of the boys, called out. "Where were ya? We came by to get air in my back tire."

"I was out on the trail. Looks like you guys are going to get some ice cream, too."

"Yeah." Both kids gazed up at him, eyes bright. "You gonna be at the garage later?"

"Only for my friends." He winked at them. "After

I'm done with my cone, I'll head over and unlock the doors, okay?''

"That'd be great, Zach. Karen, can we pet your horse? Does she bite?''

"No. She likes her nose rubbed.''

The boys turned their attention to the mare, who liked children and noticed right away they had candy in their pockets.

"See what a great guy I am?'' Zach whispered in Karen's ear. "Even kids like me.''

"Because you have the only air pump in town.'' She swung her leg over Star's rump, starting to dismount.

His fingers closed around her forearms, stopping her. His touch was both gentle and steadfast, and it rocked her to the core.

"Let me help you. It's a long way down and I wouldn't want you to fall.''

"I've been riding since I was four. I think I can dismount all by myself.''

"Humor me. I had that scare today, imagining you crashing to the ground, breaking bones. I'd feel safer if I lifted you down.''

"Zach, I don't think—''

"Look at this loose gravel. It would really hurt if you fell. Lacerate your knees. Cut up your pretty hands.'' Trouble flashed in his eyes.

"I'm not going to fall.''

"Let's be safe rather than sorry.'' His grip tightened.

She slid off the mare's back and into his arms as if she belonged there. As if she always would.

Just friends, she vowed. Friendly was all she wanted to feel for him.

But this was more. Much more.

Time froze, the world faded away and she was suspended in the air, held safe by Zach's strength. Awareness tingled through her like a buzz from an electric current. A jolt of realization surged through her so strong, it could have been lightning from the sky.

Zach's eyes darkened and his gaze focused on her mouth. He lowered her to the ground, but she couldn't feel the solid earth beneath her feet, or the sun on her back or the wind in her hair. All she knew was that Zach was holding her, his rock-solid hands banding her arms, his steady gaze holding hers.

Her heart raced, her stomach tumbled and she couldn't breathe.

Zach motioned toward the little window where the two boys were collecting their double cones. "We're next."

"Hi, Karen. Zach." The waitress behind the window smiled and lifted one brow. "Good to see you two together. What can I get you?"

"I'd like a double chocolate cone dip." Zach leaned on the window's ledge. "Karen?"

He appeared as if everything were normal, as if nothing had changed, as if he had no idea what she was feeling.

Karen cleared her throat, managing to speak. She got her order right—at least she thought she did—and reached into her pocket. Zach had already paid. Before she could say anything more, he was handing her a butterscotch sundae with two red plastic spoons.

"There's shade over there." Zach pushed his bike to where a stand of trees shaded a few tables and benches in a patch of mown grass. He gestured toward a lonely table. "How about here?"

She nodded, and he leaned his bike against a tree trunk. Keeping hold of Star's reins, she sat on the wooden table, propping her feet on the dusty bench. Star sidled close. Cradling her bowl of ice cream, Karen watched Zach out of the corner of her eye. Furtively, as if she were afraid to look at him directly.

I *am* falling for him. The realization boomed through the stormy confusion of her mind.

A place deep in her heart warmed when he settled on the table beside her, his elbow nudging hers.

Karen thought about inching away so their arms weren't touching but stayed right where she was. Being this close to him was nice. Comforting. He was steel-strong and she liked it. She didn't want to, but she did.

"Two spoons?" he asked, friendly as always.

"One for me, one for Star."

"You really feed your horse ice cream?" He watched, shaking his head, as the mare neatly lipped the treat from the plastic spoon Karen held out.

"Star and I used to do everything together when I

was little. It was a sweet time, riding to town for ice cream and candy, exploring trails in the foothills, playing in the river. You're a boy so you probably don't understand a little girl's love for her horse.''

"I had a bike. I loved my bike." How he was teasing her!

"That's not the same." Star nudged Karen's cheek with affection, and she rubbed the mare's nose. "Little girls grow up and don't have all the time in the world to ride through the fields with their best friend or share a sundae."

"Grown-up girls *could* make time for their horses."

"I try, but it isn't easy. It's sad when I see her in the pasture every morning, watching me leave for work. I'd always figured I'd be married and have kids by now—a little girl who would take over feeding Star ice cream and racing her through the fields."

"You dated Jay a long time. Why did you wait so long for him to propose? A lot of girls I know have a time line. After a year of dating, they want to see a diamond ring sparkling on their finger."

"Maybe I wasn't so sure about the man. Or what I deserved." Karen dipped Star's spoon into the ice cream. "That hurt to admit."

"I guess. Maybe the real question is, how could Jay deserve you? Or how could I, for that matter. You're a really nice person, Karen. I'm surprised half the guys in the county aren't trying to knock me over and take my place sitting right here beside you."

"Nice. I thought I told you not to use that word. Maybe I'm not nice."

"What do you mean? You're one of the nicest women in town."

"That's not a compliment. Nice means dependable. Reliable. Boring. It means the kind of woman a man settles for."

"The secret of Jay is revealed." Zach's gaze narrowed as he munched on his cone. "That's why you called off the wedding."

Pain knotted in her chest and she dipped her spoon into the gooey ice cream.

"He's a fool, if you ask me. Anyone with eyes can see that you're no woman to settle for." Zach leaned closer and slipped his arm around her back, strong and comforting and more wonderful than she could ever dream. "A man doesn't settle for a woman like you. He gets lucky. Very lucky."

"You're trying to charm me and it isn't working."

"Fine, then. You're not nice. You're the meanest person I've ever met." He tried to tease and failed.

Memories of how he'd almost kissed her on the lips flashed through her mind. He was so close, she could feel the rise and fall of his chest. See the flicker of want in his gaze.

Her mouth tingled. She wondered—just for a second—what it would feel like to be kissed by him. Would she know the instant their lips met, if he was the one she'd been wishing for? A man who could love her truly?

"Hey, Zach!" Little Tommy Clemmins shouted across the gravel lot. "Are you goin' to the garage now?"

"I guess I *am* done with my ice cream." Zach flashed her an apologetic grin, as if he were perfectly aware of how attracted she was to him. "Why don't you stay here in the shade, Karen? I'll be right back."

"Think I'll wait around for you, huh?"

"Yeah, I do." Far too sure of himself, he hopped off the table and grabbed his bike, running. In one smooth movement he swung onto the seat, pedaling easily, to catch up with the boys.

Karen watched, mesmerized, unable to look away.

They rode three abreast between the curb and the road, the rise and fall of their voices fading. They pulled into the shop's lot, the boys dragging their bikes up to the door.

Zach dug through his pocket and searched through his key ring. He looked up. Across the half a block where dust eddied along the paved road, their gazes met. There was no mistaking his grin or the pull of attraction that zinged between them.

Okay, maybe I'd like falling for him. And in a big way.

But this was *Zach*. She'd known him since kindergarten, the quiet boy with the secondhand clothes and the saddest eyes she'd ever seen. Zach from high school, a little rugged, a little tough, who kept to himself and held two jobs throughout his high school years. Zach from the garage who'd bought a cup of coffee from her shop nearly every morning for the last four years.

How could a man she'd known forever suddenly seem so different? As if she'd finally met the real Zach?

"C'mon, girl." Karen let Star lick the plastic bowl clean and then she mounted up.

She nosed the mare through the parking lot toward the garage. Her pulse kicked up a faster rhythm as she approached Zach's shop.

There he was, kneeling down beside the air pump between the two little boys. He filled one tire in seconds. The kids clamored to their feet, swinging onto their bikes. Zach listened as the boys told of their latest adventure and what they were up to next.

Karen stopped Star on the sidewalk, seeing in Zach what she never had before. Forget his childhood, his vocation and even his motorcycle parked at the back of the shop.

Zachary Drake was pure kindness. He laughed with the boys and then wished them luck when they raced off.

He liked children, and he was kind to old women. He was a *good* man, heart and soul.

Just like Jay was.

And look how that turned out.

The peaceful glow she felt began to fade. Disappointment filled her, heavy like twilight.

"Hey, Karen." Zach strolled out of the building's shade. "Have any plans for tonight?"

"Gramma's taking me to Bozeman. We're going shopping at the mall."

"Definitely female territory."

"Yep, hazardous for any man." The distance between them felt so wide, and she knew the rift was in her heart.

Moments ago they'd been side by side, touching, nearly kissing. And now the sidewalk might as well be the Grand Canyon.

She kept seeing how he'd treated the boys, easygoing and kind, his eyes gleaming with a quiet hunger.

He wanted to be a father, she realized.

And the truth was, she wanted a family of her own, too. And a man to love her—*truly* love her. To hold her close, to make her laugh, to walk down the road of life at her side. Always at her side.

She had to wonder—could Zachary Drake be that man?

Chapter Eight

"Gramma, look." Karen spotted a tasteful knit shorts set hanging on the circular rack and pulled it from the display. "This would look perfect on you. What do you think?"

Gramma turned from the opposite rack. "That shade of aqua does suit me."

"You'll be beautiful in it. Want me to add it to the stack in our dressing room? I was about to make a trip anyway."

"I'll come with you. I think I'll grab me a pair of denims on the way. My, this is fun. I always hate shopping, but then, I've never bought so much in one place. Goodness, I know I ought to feel guilty, but maybe I'll take a second pair."

"Go for it." Karen took two pairs of denims from the shelf near the dressing room. "A woman deserves to treat herself now and then."

Her grandmother tugged open the wooden slatted door and led the way into the tiny mirrored room. Voices rose over the top of the dressing room partitions, and the frustrated voices of teenager and mother filled the air in a brief argument.

"For me the tables are reversed," Gramma confessed in a whisper. "Your mother can't believe how I'm dressing. She thinks I ought to act my age."

"You *are* acting your age," Karen assured her, pushing the door shut. "There's no reason why you can't change your image now and then. You're still the gramma I love."

"As I love you, my precious girl. Thank you for coming along with me to help." She glanced around the tiny room where the hooks on the walls bulged with clothes. "This is too much. I don't know where to start."

"That's because you've never shopped with Michelle. Luckily, I have. There's a system." Karen set down her purse next to the already-overflowing shopping bags on the floor and began organizing the hangers. "Jeans first. Those are always the most frustrating. Try this style."

"I've always wanted to own a pair of these. Norman thought they were what forward women wore, not the mother of his children. So I wore dresses." Gramma stepped out of her shorts and reached for the denims. "I saw you in town today, riding that horse of yours. Was I right about taking time off to get some sunshine?"

"You were absolutely wrong. I should have been doing the bookkeeping and serving iced mochas instead of paying Michelle to drive away my customers."

"Don't try fooling me, sweetie." Gramma buttoned the waistband and twirled in front of the mirror. "Oh, my. Is that really me?"

"Yes." Karen felt joy creep into her heart, and she wrapped her arms around her grandmother. "You've always been beautiful, and you always will be. No matter what you wear."

"I sure look modern in these jeans."

Karen bit her lip to keep from laughing. "That means you're taking both pairs?"

"Yes!" Gramma beamed at her reflection.

"Then let's try these shirts." Karen unbuttoned a snazzy silk garment from its plastic hanger. "This color is going to look great on you."

"You are in a good mood, aren't you? I'm so pleased you took some time for yourself."

"Until I take a look at my books and I'll change my mind."

Gramma slipped into the new garment, turning to admire the look of it in the triple mirrors. "Is your little shop really doing that poorly? You know my friends and the women's groups at church always make a point to bring their business to your doorstep."

"I know, and I appreciate their loyalty more than I can say, but profits aren't what I was hoping for."

Karen unhooked another shirt from its hanger. "Yet. But my busy season is right around the corner. As soon as there's a nip in the morning air, you watch business pick up."

"You know what you need?" Gramma pulled the second shirt over her head. "A business partner. Someone to share the workload with."

"Then it wouldn't be my shop anymore. It's sentimental, I know, but I don't want to change it too much."

Gramma tried on a third top, seconds ticking by as she studied the rose-pink knit with the sporty cut. "Does this look too young on me?"

"It looks fun, casual and tasteful. I've seen your friend Nora Greenley in something similar."

"Then put this on the 'buy' pile, too, dear. I have another thought about your little shop."

"I don't want you to worry about my business."

"That's a lot of responsibility to shoulder for a girl your age."

"In a few years I'll be thirty. I think I'm old enough for a little responsibility."

"But when you started the shop, you weren't alone. You had your sister. Comrades-in-arms, I called you. Everywhere she went, you went. I thought of her today, simply couldn't help it, when I saw you riding horseback through town. Memories rushed back of the two of you, as identical as sisters could be, riding side by side on your mares, giggling and talking in the way little girls do. Hair in ponytails and as sun-browned as can be. You looked happy today.''

"It's been a long time since I took Star to town for ice cream. Usually I take her along the river trail so she can get a good run.''

"I bet you ordered a butterscotch sundae and shared it with her. Like always.''

"I did.'' Karen handed her grandmother a blue angora cardigan. "This will be just right when the weather turns.''

"You're changing the subject on me because you know good and well what I'm about to say next.'' Gramma's wise gaze narrowed.

"If you saw me in town getting ice cream, then you saw that I wasn't alone.''

"Zachary Drake is such a nice man. Good to the core. Sure, he got into a little trouble in his youth, but look where he came from. No father, and no mother that would make sure her kids were cared for, drunk all the time. Sad, it was. But Zach took care of the younger ones, and now he runs a good business. He's a volunteer fireman. Works in the Search and Rescue. Did you hear about that hiker he scaled a cliff to save?''

"You know I did.'' Karen added the cardigan to the growing pile. "This conversation isn't heading where I think it is, right? You're not going to mention how Lois brought more pictures of her great grandbaby to your last meeting.''

"I'm shocked. I wasn't about to mention one word

about marriage and babies. Only what a wonderful choice in friends you have.''

"I don't believe you.'' Karen laughed.

"I only have your best interests at heart. He's a handsome one, and that never hurts in a marriage.''

"See? You said that awful *M* word.''

"I know you want to get married.''

"One day. To the right man.'' Karen unhooked the shorts set from the stubborn hangers, refusing to look at her grandmother in case she guessed the truth. Karen wasn't going to let anyone know she was interested in Zachary Drake. ''According to my sisters, I need a rebound relationship. To help me get over Jay.''

"Those girls read too many magazines.'' Gramma laughed, slipping out of her jeans. ''Fold these up for me. Heavens! Look at that pile. This makeover is going to put me in the poorhouse!''

"But think how good you'll look going there. Can we stop talking about Zach?''

"I have only one more thing to say about Zach, so I'll just say it. He's a nice man and as good as gold. He serves his church and his community, he's an honest businessman and kids love him. Bet you noticed that.''

"Just how long were you spying on me this afternoon?''

"I could see you from the coffee shop window.'' Gramma chuckled. ''Okay, end of subject. I have another thought on your business troubles.''

"My business troubles aren't yours."

Gramma admired the classy shorts set in the mirror, eyes sparkling, full of trouble. "What you should do is find a business partner you get along with. One who works hard, has a positive outlook on life, has money and wants what you want for the shop."

"Oh, and just where would I find this perfect partner? If you mention Zach's name, I won't speak to you for a week, and that's a promise." Karen fought to keep a straight face as she freed a summer dress from its hanger. "I mean it."

"Zach? Why, no, I'm not that sneaky." Laughing, Gramma slipped into the frothy garment. "I was talking about me."

"You?"

"I'm just spending my life sitting in my house and puttering around in my garden. Now, mind you, I love to putter and I love my home, but I've got too much time on my hands. Sure, I have my church commitments and that helps, but I'd like to be a business-woman."

"No."

"I know how to mix up those fancy coffee drinks, plus I make a mean sandwich. I get compliments. Admit it."

"Filling in now and then for me is one thing, but you're retired. You don't need the stress or the responsibility of a business, believe me."

"What I want is to feel like I'm making a difference with my life. You're working yourself to the bone trying to keep the shop you love afloat, and I need something to do. Will you help me?''

"You know I will." Karen's heart twisted with grief at the lonely sound twisted up in her grandmother's words. "But the last thing I want is your money. You've given me a car, for heaven's sake, and I'm going to have to pay you for it, you know. Helping me with my business is way too much—"

"You owe me nothing for the car, and as for the business, maybe I have selfish motives. Maybe I won't be helping you as much as I want to help myself." Gramma's chin lifted.

"Why the shop? Maybe there's other things you'd like to do."

"Sure, I can find something else to do with my days, but what I want most of all is to spend a part of them with you. That would make me the happiest, working in our pleasant little shop. I don't want to, but I will beg if I have to."

Now what did she do? Karen prayed for the right words to obliterate her grandmother's pain—and the guidance to lower her own pride. "How about a test run before we make it official? To make sure you won't have regrets."

"I knew I could win you over." Gramma pressed a kiss to her cheek. "Now, let me change out of this heavenly dress, which I absolutely must have. No, I'm not even going to look at the price tag. And then you and I are going to go check out the coffee shop on the other side of mall. There has to be some more trade secrets we can learn. To think, I'm going to be a businesswoman!''

As good as gold. That's how her grandmother had described the man who was rapping his knuckles on her shop's back door. As he did every morning.

Remembering the kiss that had almost happened, Karen's fingers felt jerky as she waved him in.

He brought the brightness of the morning with him. ''Hi, gorgeous. I'm in desperate need of caffeine and figured only you could help me.''

''For the right price.''

''I knew it was too good to be true. Buy a girl ice cream and she starts taking liberties with you. Like overcharging for her fancy coffee.'' He set his thermos on the counter. ''Fill 'er up for me with regular leaded.''

''Sure. Let me get some drip started. It'll take about five minutes.''

''I can wait. The fish aren't going anywhere.''

She grabbed the bag of freshly ground beans from the freezer. ''Heading out to the river?''

''Yep, got to catch me some dinner. My refrigerator's empty.''

''The grocery store is right around the corner. Their frozen section is stocked.''

''What? And go to all that trouble of fighting the crowds for food? Not me. I'm going to go catch my chow the real man's way.''

''How's that—shopping for frozen dinners?''

"I never should have told you about those. I'm leaving now."

"Have you ever actually caught a fish? Or do you just sit there and watch the water stream by?"

"I can't believe this. My favorite person in town is mocking me. Casting doubt on my manly fishing skills." He shook his head, feigning disapproval. "I'm going to start buying my coffee at the diner."

She poured water into the machine and flipped the switch. "Manly fishing skills? Women can be just as good fishers as men. In fact, I always caught the most when Dad took me and Allison."

"Am I hearing this right? Are you challenging me to a fishing contest?" Zach propped his elbows on the counter. "If you think you're better, then prove it. We'll make a fishing date, just you and me. An early-morning contest to see who's the best."

"I haven't fished since I was eight." Karen marched into the kitchen, far too aware of Zach's gaze on her back. Far too aware of everything about him.

No one had ever made her laugh the way Zach did. Or made her feel happy and full of warmth, like the sun was right in the middle of her chest, lighting her up from the inside.

Gramma straightened from the oven, a heavy muffin tin in both hands. "These are perfect if I do say so myself. I noticed handsome Zach wandered in."

"You were spying on me." Karen grabbed a clean plate from the stack on the counter and stole a plump blueberry muffin from the cooling racks. "Zach and I are friends."

"Clearly."

"I see that look in your eye. The one that says you know better than me. Well, I don't care what my sisters say. I'm not ready for a rebound relationship."

"I'm sure you're right." Gramma transferred the steaming banana muffins from the tin to the cooling racks. "I say Zach's a nice guy, but he's just like Jay. Too lukewarm to lose your heart to. My advice is to keep away from a relationship that will only hurt you in the end."

"Reverse psychology. That's not going to work, either."

"What? I know nothing about psychology." All innocence, Gramma continued to work. "I'm simply saying that we're in this together. We've got to make this place profitable for that big payment due next month. I can't have my partner falling in love and neglecting business."

"I don't believe you. Do you need help?"

"No, you go take those muffins to Zach and make sure you don't flirt with him. It would be unprofessional."

Karen rolled her eyes. "I minored in psychology. I know what you're up to."

"I have no idea what you're talking about."

Shaking her head, Karen pushed through the swinging door. The first thing she saw was Zach, one elbow propped on the counter and looking more handsome than he'd been yesterday—than she'd ever seen him.

How did a man become more and more good-looking? And why?

Okay, she knew. She was falling for him. Hard and fast, and she couldn't seem to help it.

"I heard Helen's voice. Is she helping you out this morning?"

"She talked me into a possible partnership." Karen grabbed a bag from under the counter and snapped it open. "She wants to be half owner."

"No kidding. How did that come about?"

"She played on my sympathies. And if I hadn't caved in, then she would have worked on my guilt." Karen slipped the muffins into the paper bag and folded it neatly. "She claims that she sits alone in her house all day and needs something to do."

"Hey, Helen. You should have gone into business with me. You could be doing oil changes right now."

The door pushed open, showing a slice of the kitchen behind the well-dressed woman holding an empty muffin tin. "Why, Zachary Drake, I didn't know you were in the market for a *partner*." Gramma winked.

Mortified, Karen shoved the muffin bag at Zach. "Gramma! Zach doesn't need a partner. He's perfectly happy being a sole proprietor."

"That's not entirely true." Zach lifted one brow, trouble shaping his saucy grin. "I've been on my own a long time. The right investor comes along with a pretty smile and I could consider a merger.''

"Zach!'' Karen threw a napkin at him. "You know my grandmother is talking about marriage.''

"Of course he does, honey,'' Gramma answered. "And what a pleasure it is to cast my gaze on a man who isn't afraid of commitment.''

"That's it. You're fired.'' Karen grabbed Zach's thermos.

"She's only kidding, Zach.'' Gramma set down her tin and padded closer. "She's grumpy. She works all the time. She took a few hours off yesterday, and apparently it wasn't enough.''

"I'm *not* grumpy. Not until you started mentioning mergers.'' Karen filled the thermos.

"I understand too well,'' Zach answered, all charm. "I get that way myself when I don't take enough time off. All work and no play.''

"It's not how the good Lord intended it,'' Gramma agreed.

"You two are conspiring.'' Karen capped the thermos, daring to face them. "Zach, here's your coffee. Happy fishing. Gramma, we've got the last batch of muffins to finish. We open in fifteen minutes.''

"Yeah, Helen,'' Zach drawled. "Look at the stampede approaching the front door. It's going to be a madhouse.''

"Yep, looks like they're getting ready to beat down the door,'' Gramma quipped. "There's not a soul in sight. Should pick up after Labor Day. Come to think of it, I think this is the perfect time for Karen to get out. You used to love to fish.''

''Just how much did you eavesdrop while you were making those muffins?''

''I heard everything.'' Gramma patted Zach's hand. ''Be a gentleman and do an old woman a favor. Take my Karen with you this morning. Let her get some fresh air. It's the best thing for her.''

''Gramma, you're not a matchmaking service. Zach, you don't want me intruding—''

''Sure I do.'' Zach grabbed his thermos. ''Karen, come with me. We might as well have that contest right now.''

''No.'' She couldn't just leave. ''It will be a quiet morning, but it's Gramma's first real day—''

''You know you want to,'' her grandmother whispered in her ear. ''I'll be fine, and you know that, too. You take today off, and I'll take tomorrow off. Is that a deal?''

''Are you sure? I don't want to run out on you.''

''This is the reason for having a business partner. Now go and have fun. Isn't that the point of a rebound relationship?''

''A rebound relationship?'' Zach quirked one brow, trying not to laugh. ''Well, I've been worse. Come on, gorgeous. I've got an extra pole at the shop I'll let you use. I'll even share some of my coffee.''

''That's technically my coffee, since you didn't pay for it.''

''Yes, but possession is nine-tenths of the law.''

Zach held the door for her, his hand skimming her elbow.

Karen shivered all the way to her soul.

It was a beautiful morning. He was self-employed and there was no work waiting for him in the shop. It wasn't every day that a man got this lucky. Zach couldn't help but give a quick, silent prayer of thanks as he pulled his pickup into the shade of old cottonwoods.

"Listen to the river." He set the parking brake. The ping-ping of the engine cooling contrasted with the peaceful sounds of nature. "It's saying, 'Karen, leave your troubles behind.'"

"Funny, I only hear a faint gurgle. Maybe the river is saying, 'Karen, you will catch more fish than Zachary.'"

"You're a riot."

He could sit here looking at her all day. She was as refreshing to his spirit as morning, and he wanted nothing more than to pull her into his arms and hold her.

He wanted to have the right to kiss her, gentle and softly, so she would know his true feelings. Deep and tender feelings that no words could describe.

She seemed shy as she reached for the thermos and the small paper bag that proclaimed, Field of Beans, across the front in swirling green script.

"I'll give you my best fishing rod," he told her.

"When I win, I don't want you to accuse me of being unfair."

"When *you* win? Ha! I sure hope you're not a poor sport, because you're going to lose." Golden tendrils escaped from her ponytail and fluttered in front of her eyes.

He brushed the gossamer wisps back into place, trying not to think too much about how satiny her skin felt or how silky her hair was.

"Your hands were full," he explained. "I was only being gentlemanly. I wouldn't want you to fall out of my truck because you couldn't see where you were going."

"I appreciate it. Are you ready to go fishing?" She didn't move.

Neither did he.

This is what it would be like if they were a couple. It was a big leap thinking of the two of them as a couple, but why not? Maybe they could be.

Just treat her well. Show her what a nice guy I can be. Twice as nice as Jay. What was it she'd told him? *Nice means dependable. The kind of woman a man settles for.*

One thing was for sure, *he'd* never let Karen doubt how special she was to him.

She walked beside him down the bank. "I'd forgotten how peaceful the river is in the mornings."

"That's why I fish. There's nothing like a quiet morning listening to the river to put things in perspective. Here we are." He leaned the rods against a tree trunk and set the tackle box in the spindly grasses. "I've never shared my fishing spot with a woman before."

"Should I be honored?"

"Sure. If you like this, I should take you to my favorite hideaway. As long as you're willing to climb a mountain to get there."

She uncapped the thermos. "What's that supposed to mean?"

"There's nothing like sitting on the peak you've scaled. With the sweat trickling down your back and your muscles so exhausted they burn. After you've picked your way up a thousand feet of sheer rock, problems don't seem so big and a lot easier to solve. You feel like there's just you, the mountain and the sky, and you're a lot closer to God." He took the thermos from her.

"I've heard rumors that you're a good mountain climber. You climb, you bike, you hike and you fish. Is there anything you can't do?"

"Cook, dust and sew. Other than that, I'm your man."

You could be. Karen caught the words before they spilled across her tongue. She wasn't ready for these feelings, but she couldn't stop them.

Zach poured coffee into the shallow cup, steam lifting in foggy curls. He offered it to her, his silence as powerful as his presence.

The admiration she'd always felt for him had

changed. Denying it wouldn't help. She had to acknowledge their relationship had irrevocably changed.

They could be more than friends. So much more.

She took the cup, feeling the warmth though the
plastic.

"Enjoy the view." He tucked the thermos into the
grass next to fishing poles. "I'll run to the truck and
grab the waders."

"Waders? I thought we were fishing from the
bank."

"Surprise." He jogged easily through the golden
grasses and out of sight. Leaving her alone with her
coffee, her awakening heart and a growing question.
Did Zach look at her and see a dependable, take-for-
granted kind of girl?

She balanced the cup on top of a rock and reached
for the tackle box. She opened the lid, amazed at the
tidy compartments of neatly tied flies, each a combination of knotted fish line, yarn and plastic buglike
bobbles.

"You're laughing." Zach dropped a pair of boots
beside her. "What's so funny about my tackle box?"

"You put hours into this. Look, organized by color
of yarn. By the type of bobble and hook. Your apartment is a mess and you can't cook, but you have time
for this?"

"A man always has time for what's truly important." He knelt beside her and lifted a fly from the
tray. "I only have one pair of waders, but I keep my

fire boots in the back of the truck. They should work.''

''Thanks, but these are huge.'' Karen moved away to inspect what he'd brought. ''The good news is that I don't have to take my shoes off. Look.''

He didn't see the too-big boots. He saw *her*. Like an angel on earth, warm and sparkling. She made him feel both vulnerable and strong, tender and fierce all at once. He wanted to protect her and he wanted to love her for the rest of his life.

She was everything he'd ever wanted. Home and family. Belonging and love. And…just Karen. He'd always had a crush on the quiet gentle girl who was way out of his reach.

Not anymore. Her smile deepened when she looked at him. She was stardust straight from heaven, and he couldn't believe she wanted to be with him.

Unaware, she took the pole from him and clomped toward the river, wearing the heavy boots that went to her midthighs.

He grabbed his fishing pole, pulled his waders to his knees and splashed into the water after her.

''Are you ready?'' she challenged with her rod raised, hook dangling above the rippling water. ''Stand back. It's been a long time since I've cast.''

''That's comforting. If you hook me, I don't count as a fish.''

''Why not? We're not going by weight of the catch?'' She leaned the pole back to her shoulder, swinging the hook far behind her. With a flick of her slender wrist, the fly snapped through the air, skimming the river's shimmering surface.

"Not bad for a girl. Now watch the master." He cast, satisfaction filling him when he saw the lure slice into the water. "Perfection."

"Not bad for a boy." She reeled in, the fly cutting toward them against the current.

She recast and silence fell between them. A contented peace that felt like forever.

Don't just stand there, Zach. You're alone with the girl. A man doesn't get a chance like this every day.

He edged closer.

She flashed him a smile. "I'm having trouble."

"Good thing I'm here. Since I'm also an expert fisherman, I've got the experience to help you out." That made her chuckle. "You've got a tangle, that's all."

"Did I mess up your reel?"

"Not a chance. There's a knot in the line. Look. It must have happened in the water." He pulled out his pocketknife.

Keeping his pole tucked against his side, he leaned closer to Karen. Close enough to smell the baby shampoo in her hair. That was his favorite scent, he decided. Especially since she was his favorite girl.

"Let me just cut this off here." He inserted the tip of his knife beneath the knotted fishing line, bringing his forehead to hers.

So close. He wanted to kiss her. To show her how he felt and what he wanted to give her—protection, commitment and tenderness. That's what he wanted her to see whenever she looked at him.

"There." The line came free. "Let me tie the hook for you."

"I can do it."

His fingers were fumbling, but he got the job done. "There. No fish is safe now."

Instead of releasing the line, he moved closer.

Karen felt anticipation zip through her. The river's current tugged at her legs, keeping her a little off balance. She wobbled and didn't know if it was because of the river or her feelings for Zach.

He leaned closer and she forgot to breathe. Her eyelids fluttered shut as their lips met in a sweet brush that left her trembling.

How could it be that one chaste kiss could hold so much tenderness?

Zach broke away and she opened her eyes. They were still standing in the river with the sun glinting on the water and the cottonwoods whispering with the breezes—an ordinary morning that was not the same as it had been five seconds before.

Everything had changed.

Zach's hand cupped the side of her face. A gentle, comforting touch that made her heart ache with hope. With a dream of what could be.

She leaned into his touch and welcomed his kiss. The ache within her intensified, making her hurting and happy all at once. Sweet love for him filled her up until she couldn't breathe, until she couldn't tell up from down or feel the rocky riverbed at her feet.

"Your nose is cold," he told her, chuckling, and leaned his forehead to hers to prolong the moment of closeness. "Want me to fetch the thermos?"

She grabbed hold of his arm to steady herself. Heat flamed her cheeks, and how could she tell him how she felt? That he'd affected her so much she was wobbly on her feet?

A tug on the pole jerked her forward. Was it a fish? Before she could set the hook, she lost her balance and tumbled against Zach's solid chest. His arms banded around her, but it was too late. Her feet lost contact with the riverbed and gravity pulled her down.

She fell with a splash into the river. Water rushed over her and the cold stung her skin. She sputtered, fighting for the surface, and then Zach tumbled into the river beside her bobbing for air.

"Are you all right?" He half swam, half climbed toward her. "Did you hit your head on any rocks?"

Concern furrowed into his brow as he caught her with his strong but gentle hands. "I don't see any bruises. Any lumps? Do you know what day it is?"

"I'm fine, Zach." Her voice came breathy and thin. She stumbled over a rock and pain shot through her bare foot. "I lost my shoes and your boots, but I didn't let go of your pole."

Zach dipped beneath the water and came up with one of her slip-on sneakers. He went down again and surfaced with the other. "What happened? Looks like you lost your hook."

"Guess I got a bite and it took me by surprise." She stared down at the fishing rod, the line a loose tangle. "He got away."

"No, he didn't." Zach swiped water from her face with the side of his thumb. "I've been here all along."

He kissed her again, briefly, sweetly until her toes curled. Then he took her hand.

"I'm holding on to you this time," he whispered in her ear. "I don't want you to fall over, since my kisses have such an impact on you."

"It wasn't you, it was a fish," she alibied as he took her hand, helping her through the current, his strength an anchor that saw her safely to shore.

Chapter Nine

"There you are. I was beginning to worry. Let me help you with those." Holding open her screen door, Gramma wrestled a grocery bag from Karen's arms. "You didn't need to buy all this."

"I didn't want to empty your pantry. Zach helped me, too." Karen stumbled into her grandmother's cozy kitchen, nearly dropping the heavy bags. "Did you make sense of those financial statements I gave you?"

"I've been looking at them all afternoon until my eyes went blurry. I wanted to blame my bifocals, but I know good and well I was nothing but confused. Those classes I signed up for at the university ought to help straighten me out."

"I think Zach told me he did the same thing." Karen set the heavy grocery bags on the counter. "Now he does his own books."

"Zach said so, huh?" Gramma's eyes twinkled.

"I see what you're thinking, so don't even start." Karen shrugged the purse strap from her shoulder. "It isn't any of your business."

"How could it be, since the two of you are only *friends?*"

"Exactly."

It wasn't a lie, not really. They *were* friends. Then why did the tingle of his kiss remain? So, maybe he could be more than just a friend. "He's going to be really happy that you made your taco cheese and macaroni casserole just for him."

"We have to pay back that man somehow. He's always doing for me, I swear. This afternoon while you were at the bank he stopped by to check on my new car. Says he wanted to keep an eye on the oil, since it's important to a new engine. Imagine that. Didn't charge me a penny."

"Imagine that." Karen reached into the nearest grocery bag, hiding a smile. "So, you're trying to tell me what a nice guy he is."

"Good husband material. Not that you're looking." Gramma set a clean saucepan on the stove. "But believe me, some other girl is going to notice. She'll snatch him up, and then it'll be too late for you."

"That's a risk I'm willing to take." Karen emptied the grocery bag.

"After he was done checking the engine, you know what he did? Told me something shocking. Young lady, you're keeping a secret from your grand-mother.''

"Secret? What secret?"

"To think I have to hear about this from my mechanic and not my granddaughter. Not one bit." Gramma waved a spatula.

Heat burned Karen's face. "I can't believe it. Zach told you?"

"He surely did. Told me right there in front of my dearest friends. Nora was appalled, and she wasn't the only one."

That didn't sound like Zach. There was no way he would have broadcast news of their kiss to some of the most respected women in their church!

"Just what did he tell you?"

"About the radiator, of course. How it steamed on the way home from the car dealership, and how you had to walk to town."

Relief left her dizzy. "I didn't tell you because I didn't want your feelings hurt. I'm grateful for the car."

"I told Zachary *he* was at fault. A mechanic ought to be responsible for his own shoddy work." Gramma winked. "I told him you would bring the car in for a new radiator."

"I know what you're up to." Karen headed to the pantry. "You're going to try and pay for the repairs and I'm not going to let you—no, don't argue. I don't need a new radiator right away. He fixed it for now."

"You'd better have him give the engine a thorough

check. Make sure there isn't any trouble lurking beneath the hood. After all, if he's just a *friend,* you won't mind spending more time with him.''

Karen slipped into the large pantry, stocked with shelves of food and jars of homemade jellies. She tucked the folded bags into place. ''Are you trying to play matchmaker?''

''Absolutely not! I'm not one of those meddling grandmothers who thinks they know what's best for their beloved granddaughters.''

''That's good to hear. Because the last thing Zach and I need right now is a matchmaker.''

''I understand completely. I'm glad you and that nice young man are only *friends* because you and I have a business to run.''

Karen struggled not to laugh. It wasn't hard to see right through Gramma's strategy.

''Get me the flour canister and a package of noodles while you're over there.''

''Sure.'' Karen peeked over her shoulder. Gramma wasn't looking, so she tugged the money from her jeans pocket. The same hundred-dollar bills Zach had given her for her old car.

She snatched a battered tin from the top shelf and carefully pried off the lid. ''Since tomorrow is Labor Day, it should be quiet at the shop, too. Did you want to close early? I did last year.''

''That's fine by me. What are you doing in there? I need the flour.''

''I'm coming.'' Karen tucked the money inside and

replaced Gramma's secret money tin. It wasn't close to what she owed for the car, but it was a start.

The long day made his apartment seem more homey than usual. Zach tossed his keys on the table. A message light blinked in the darkness. His personal line, not the shop phone.

Did he dare hope it was Karen? He'd thought of her all day. Images of her accepting his kiss and reaching out for him when she fell. The telltale blush on her cheeks had told him she felt the spark between them, too.

He had a chance with her. A real, honest-to-goodness chance.

He hit the play button and flicked on lights as the tape rewound. "Zach, this is your sister. Just checking in on you. Are you eating right? I worry. Talk to you later."

He liked the happiness in his sister's voice. He'd give her a call as soon as—

"Zach?" Another message started. "This is your mother."

His emotions took a nosedive. Why did his hands shake every time he thought of that woman?

"I need five hundred dollars. I'm in a real fix and I don't know who to call—"

Zach pressed the stop button, cutting off the slurred speech. The thought of her filled him with shame, the old shame that he'd fought all his life. The humiliation of being Sylvia Drake's boy, the woman without a shred of dignity, who spent her life at the Bulldog Tavern, too drunk to care how she behaved or with whom.

Whenever he thought of her, the hungry little boy he'd been didn't seem too far away.

Don't go there. He squeezed his eyes shut against the images of his childhood. He didn't need to remember.

He'd send her the money because it would keep her away.

A knock at the door startled him. He yanked open the door. "Karen."

"Hi, stranger. I've been trying to get a hold of you all evening." She smiled at him over the top of two heavy-looking grocery sacks. "I finally gave up and decided to leave these in the freezer at the shop when I saw your light."

"I'm glad you came by. Let me take these for you." He avoided looking at her as he took both bags. "What do you have in here? These weigh a ton."

"A surprise for you, courtesy of my grandmother and me. Thought you could use some real food."

He saw the foil-wrapped plates, and the faint scent of Helen's taco cheese and macaroni casserole made his mouth water. "Why did you do this? You didn't have to."

"We wanted to. We made them easy to freeze, since you're used to frozen dinners. You can nuke them any time you want, and guess what? They're good for you."

"Did you put any green stuff in there like broccoli or green beans or spouts?"

"No, you're safe. Although Gramma did dice and cook carrots. Before you complain, she smothered them in this buttery sauce and said you'd like it. Carrots *are* orange."

"That grandmother of yours is sly, trying to trick me into eating vegetables." Although he was teasing, his chest tightened until he couldn't breathe.

He turned away and set the bags on the counter. There had to be two dozen dinners inside the grocery bags, each carefully prepared and proportioned.

This was the kindest thing anyone had done for him in a long time.

"Gramma offered to give you cooking lessons, since she has to keep her favorite mechanic in good health." Karen leaned against his counter, an angel in a blue T-shirt and jeans, her hair braided, with little wisps framing her face.

He loved this woman. With his whole heart. All his life he'd admired her from afar. Untouchable Karen McKaslin, a wealthy rancher's daughter.

And now that he knew her better, knew who she was inside, how easily she laughed, how gently she loved, he didn't know what to do. Did he reach for her and hold her? Did he tell her how he felt?

They'd never spoken of their relationship. He was afraid to break the spell by asking her, as if that would make her wake up from a dream and see not the man he'd worked to be, but Sylvia Drake's kid—someone she would never truly love.

Then she smiled at him, genuinely, from her soul. "Aren't you going to put them in your freezer? Gramma was afraid you wouldn't have room, but I told her about the hot dog story. There's no way you have anything but ice in your freezer."

"You're wrong about that, gorgeous. I do, too, have something in here." He jerked open the freezer door. "Empty ice trays."

"I knew it." Loaded down with plates, she shouldered up to him. "We never did determine who was the better fisherman."

"I thought I was." He took the plates from her and began stocking his freezer.

"Why you? You didn't catch a fish. I hooked one, I think, but it got away. That makes it a draw."

"A draw? No way. I'm not the one who fell into the river, so that means I'm the best."

"I was wearing your enormous boots. They made me trip. I was at a disadvantage."

"Maybe we'll have to have another contest." Uncertainty flickered in his stomach. Did he ask her for a date?

"Another contest? Maybe." She brushed her fingertips along his jaw, a brief contact, and then she moved away. "This time I get to choose what we do."

"Wait, I already know what you're going to say.

No way am I going horseback riding with you. I think those creatures are best left alone in their fields.''

"What kind of attitude is that for an adventurous guy like you? You can borrow Michelle's horse, and I'll teach you everything you need to know."

"Like how to fall? Trying to put me at a disadvantage, aren't you? Well, you should know that I'm a natural-born athlete." He caught her hand in his. "Prepare to lose and lose big because I've seen you ride, and I have to say you weren't very good at it."

"That's because you scared my horse." Her fingers twined around his, holding tight.

Holding on to him.

Something about her simply made all his doubts fade. Made him feel like a better man than he was.

He followed her to the door. "I'd better walk you to your car. This town is a wild place at night. A girl has to be careful."

"I could use the protection. This *is* a dangerous place."

Not a car passed on the street, and the shops were silent. Zach felt better, stronger, because there wasn't a safer place than this tiny town in the middle of Montana—Karen just wanted him with her.

He escorted her to the classic Ford gleaming in the starlight. "I guess I'll see you at church tomorrow. Any chance you'd sit with me?"

"It's a good possibility." She waited while he opened her car door. "It's always good for my reputation to be seen with a handsome man."

She didn't let go of him, and his heart started pounding like a jackhammer.

He brushed her cheek with his lips, breathing in the scent of her shampoo. "I'll see you in the morning."

"I'll have your coffee ready."

He shut the door for her. The rolled-down window framed her, and he was jealous of the starlight bold enough to touch her face.

She turned the key. There was a click. The car didn't start.

"Oh, no. This can't be happening. This car worked for Gramma. Never broke down on her once."

"I'll take a look." He circled around the front fender and then disappeared from her view as he popped the hood.

She leaned out the window. "Want me to try again?"

"No. It's the starter. I can fix it tonight if you want to wait, but it'll take a while."

He looked tired. She'd heard about the multicar accident on the highway south to Yellowstone today and figured he'd been called in to help. It must have been a hard day.

She got out of the car and handed him the keys. "I'll call home. Someone can come get me."

"No need. Hop in the truck and I'll take you. For the right fee."

"You're going to charge me?"

"Sure. I'll take you anywhere you want to go for a kiss."

"Wow, that's a pretty high price, but I *am* stranded here. I guess I'll just have to take you up on your offer—except for one thing. Take me on your motorcycle."

He shut the hood. "That'll cost you more."

"Name your price."

"Two kisses. If you want the scenic ride, then it's three."

"Where will the scenic ride take me?"

"Hop on and you'll find out." Zach took her hand, so gallant that he stole her breath away.

"Is this fast enough?"

Karen looked down. Big mistake. The pavement flew by at a dizzying speed. "Definitely fast enough."

"Sure about that?"

"Absolutely. This is my first motorcycle ride."

"Kind of scary and thrilling at the same time, huh?" He revved the engine, the show-off.

"Maybe you could slow down just a little." The surrounding countryside blurred. "Or a lot."

"We're not even going the speed limit. It seems faster when you look at the ground. Try closing your eyes."

"That sounds real smart. Then I won't be able to prepare for a crash."

"I never crash. Trust me."

It was hard not to. Sitting behind him with her arms wrapped around his waist, she could feel the steely strength in his back. He handled the bike with confidence.

She squeezed her eyes shut and it didn't seem as scary. "Okay, you can go faster now."

The motorcycle shot forward, skimming through the night. The roar of the engine, the whir of the wind made Karen's pulse soar. She opened one eye and then the other. It was like flying. Zach was in control, and her fear ebbed away.

They raced through the darkness with only a single headlight to show the way. The road unfolded before them, rising up and falling away like an undulating ribbon. With her arms tight around Zach, she felt safe. Safer than she'd been with anyone. Ever.

Too soon, he slowed the bike and turned off the road. He rolled to a stop and killed the engine.

Her arms were tight around his waist. She didn't want to let go and he didn't move. Finally she released him and scrambled from the bike. She slipped off the helmet, surprised the sense of safety she'd felt holding him remained.

"Do you like the scenic route?" Zach took the helmet and hung it on one handlebar. "I don't want to shortchange you. I'm a man of my word."

"I'm having a wonderful time."

"Good. Come with me." He laid his arm over her shoulder, tugging her close.

Karen cuddled against him as they walked side by side along the worn path toward the river. Night shadows cloaked the familiar landscape, making it mysterious and new.

What a magnificent night. She couldn't believe how a place she knew so well could transform before her eyes. The cottonwoods overhead whispered a solemn hymn, and the starlight cast a noble glow across the surface of the water. The river, wide and black and seemingly motionless, made no sound as they approached the bank.

"Have you ever watched a moon rise?"

"No," she confessed. "I'm usually inside this time in the evening. If I am outside, then I'm busy exercising Star."

"And you never pay attention to what's in the sky?"

"When do I have the time?" She let him help her to the ground. "Between helping Mom, and the shop—"

"Hollow excuses for a woman who named her horse Star."

"That was when I was eight and I had time to wish on the first stars of the night and watch for meteorites."

"Falling stars." He settled in the grass beside her, his arm drawing her to his side. "That's what you are to me, Karen. A falling star that landed at my side."

"Meteorites are chunks of burned rock."

"Give me a break. I'm new at this." He brushed his lips with hers. "So, I'm no poet and not much of a romantic. I took you fishing for our first date."

"That was a date? I thought it was a contest." She couldn't resist teasing him.

"You're not making this easy for me." He kissed her again, light and sweet.

"That's your second kiss. One more and my debt is paid in full."

"Those weren't real kisses. They were warm-up kisses."

"Kisses are kisses. You only have one left, buster."

"Can I negotiate for more?"

"Why should I? I'm not the kind of girl who kisses just any man for a ride on his motorcycle."

"Then I'll have to change your mind." He kissed her again, light as a breeze. "That's enough of a warm-up to appreciate the moonrise. Look."

Dazzled, she tried to focus on the eastern rim of mountains made black by the night. She caught her breath at the sight of the top point of a sickle moon nudging upward, a lone spear of light changing the landscape. The jagged mountain peaks glowed silver in the night.

She'd seen the moon before but not like this. Nothing like this.

"What do you think?" Zach's breath was warm against her ear. "Was it worth another kiss or two?"

"I only agreed to three."

"I was hoping the moon would inspire you to kiss me one more time."

"A wise plan."

The moonglow cast a silvery light over them and tonight Zach seemed changed, too. He was more than the man she'd known for years—her most loyal customer, her mechanic and a friend who made her laugh.

He was *much* more.

Like a dream, his lips met hers. His slow kiss was tender and true.

Too soon, it was over. Zach drew her into his arms and held her—simply held her—while the moon filled the sky with unquenchable light. The darkest shadows disappeared around them, and the black surface of the silent river turned silvery, reflecting the moon's glow.

All around her, the world felt different. Changed from everything she'd known before. Or maybe it was just a change within her, as if a sleeping part of her heart had awakened.

"Look at the deer." Zach lifted one hand slowly. "Right there in the grasses."

The grasses barely shifted, and Karen caught the glimpse of one white tail and then another. She didn't dare move as the doe led her fawns down to the sparkling water. The babies drank at their mother's side.

Zach's chin came to rest on the crown of Karen's head. Being close to him like this felt right. As if they'd both been led to this place.

Dear Father, tell me I'm not making a mistake, she prayed, but it was too late and she knew it. Tenderness for Zach filled her up so completely she could hardly breathe.

I love him, she thought, turning her face into his neck and letting him hold her. I love him more than I've loved anyone.

But does he love me?

That was a different question, and the answer terrified her. He liked her, he treated her well, but did he feel both enlivened and confused at the same time? Did he look at her and think, she's the one?

He tipped her head back gently. "I'm going to charge you extra for those deer."

"All these hidden charges. I might have to bring up a complaint with the chamber of commerce."

"You'd ruin my professional reputation just like that, huh? Then I'd better try to change your mind." He brushed his lips across hers once and then twice.

The third time left her feeling as if she'd touched the moon. She felt warm and was glowing. Special and so far from ordinary, dependable Karen.

Zach took her hand, as gallant as a knight of old, and helped her rise. With the breeze at her back and the stardust lighting the way, he wound his fingers through hers.

She walked slowly, the grass crackling beneath her sneakers, enjoying the weight and texture of his hand in hers. She wanted to savor this moment, to make it last, to never let it end. But too soon they were at the motorcycle. It was time to go home.

Zach stopped but didn't release her hand. "The Labor Day picnic's tomorrow. Maybe you'd consider going with me?"

"I'd love to, but I'm going with my family. Would you be brave enough to join us?"

"I sure would." He reached around her and retrieved the helmet. "I'll look forward to being seen with a pretty lady like you."

"Then I'll save you a place at my table, handsome."

He kissed her as gently as the starlight and then slipped the helmet over her head.

The ride home was silent with the moon to guide them. She held him tight and leaned her cheek on his back, her lips tingling from the memory of his sweet kisses.

Had true love finally found her?

He left her on her doorstep with a final kiss. She stood in the dark long after his bike's taillight faded in the moonlight, wishing—just wishing.

Chapter Ten

Where was he? Karen squinted through the crowd gathered in the park, where children played and smoke from the pit barbecue clouded the air. She couldn't see Zach anywhere. His pickup wasn't parked on the street. Neither was his motorcycle.

He said he'd be here, and he'd never broken a promise to her.

"Karen, your hair is getting into your face." Mom opened her purse and began sorting through it. "You need to tie it back."

"I'm fine, Mom." She was glad her mother was feeling well enough to attend the annual picnic.

"Looks like the next batch of hamburgers are done. Would you take a plate and get our meat?"

Karen wasn't fooled. Jay was at the grill, helping Dad and Pastor Bill with the barbecuing.

"Oh, here's a barrette. Clip it back for me so I can

see you.'' Mom pressed the silver barrette into Karen's palm.

''Her hair looks just fine.'' Kendra came to the rescue, bounding around the edge of the picnic table. ''But I can make it better.''

Karen handed her sister the barrette. ''Mom, I know Jay is here, so don't get your hopes up.''

''You couldn't find a nicer boy anywhere. I tell you, he's bound to go places.''

''Then he'll just have to go there with some other wife.''

''Yeah,'' Michelle piped up. ''Karen's got much better prospects.''

Mom frowned. ''What could be better than being a minister?''

''A mechanic,'' Kirby piped up from farther down the table.

Everyone laughed.

Heat splashed across Karen's face and she fought the urge to run for privacy—or cover. Heaven knew growing up with so many sisters wasn't easy. ''That is no one's business, let me remind you, no matter how nosy you all are.''

''What mechanic?'' Mom demanded. ''Girls, stop all that laughing. I can't believe what Cecilia told me was true. You're just friends with that Drake boy. Isn't that right, Karen?''

''Right.'' Whatever else they were or would become, they would always be friends first.

"Yeah, *right,*" Kendra intoned, then stepped away. "There, I'm done. Doesn't she look fabulous?"

"She's blushing," Kirby commented.

"At least that hair is out of her eyes," Mom added.

Karen rubbed her forehead. "I'm trying to remember why going to this picnic with my family was a good idea."

"Because you love us." Michelle hugged her. "I'll get the burgers and save you from dealing with Jay. C'mon, Kirby, I need help." Michelle led the way across the park.

"Sit down, honey." Mom's hand caught Karen's. "I see you looking at him. It's not too late to ask Jay for your forgiveness."

"I'm not looking at Jay." Karen kissed her Mom's cheek. "I'm glad you felt like coming today. Let me get you more lemonade."

"That would be nice."

Karen took refuge at the other end of the table. Kids playing tag raced by, screaming with delight. At the far end of the park, cheers and shouts carried on the breeze from a volleyball game in progress.

Everywhere she looked, she saw families. Hope filled her, strong as the midday sun. Maybe her dreams for a happily-ever-after were not so far away.

"Karen." John Corey, the volunteer fire chief, strolled up to her. "Zach wanted me to find you. I dropped him off at the garage a few minutes ago. We've been out all morning."

"I didn't hear anyone was missing."

"A little kid wandered away from the campsite and got herself in a little trouble. She's safe and sound now, thanks to our Zach. Or is he your Zach?" Trouble danced in the fireman's gaze. "He'll be by shortly, just so you know."

"Thanks." Karen snapped open the pitcher of lemonade.

A good man, that's what Zach is. Not only fair and kind, but concerned about everyone, neighbors and strangers alike. Her heart felt so full of love for him, she hurt with the power of it. Ached all the way to her soul.

When she glanced up, there he was at the edge of the park, waving a hello to the pastor. Dressed in jeans and a T-shirt and with his Stetson shading his eyes, he made her senses spin.

"Hello, Mrs. McKaslin. Karen, don't tell me I got here too late," he quipped, pulling her into his arms for a hug. "Where's all the food?"

"We're running late. Someone forgot the lighter fluid." She breathed in his out-of-doors and warm scent, holding him for a moment longer before she stepped away. "Gramma's not here yet, so you haven't missed the best food."

"Whew. I hurried as fast as I could to get here. I'm starving."

"Then help me take the lids off the Tupperware so we're ready to eat."

"This wouldn't be your potato salad, would it, Mrs. McKaslin? It's good to see you looking well."

"Thank you." Mom squinted at him. "It's my mother's recipe, but Michelle made it."

"Beware, she's not the best of cooks," Karen confided in him. "I tried to keep an eye on her when I was making dessert."

"Dessert? Tell me you made something with chocolate in it."

"Just for you. I was hoping that you might like my cocoa fudge cake enough to take me for another late-night bike ride."

"For the right price."

Aching tenderness filled her as she remembered last night's kisses. She knew, without words, that he was remembering, too.

"Karen, here come the girls." Mom's voice was sharper than usual. "Hurry and pass out the plates. Where's your father?"

"Talking with the other ranchers." She grabbed a bundle of paper plates from inside a grocery bag, but the small smile at the corner of her mouth remained.

Zach snapped a lid off another container—macaroni salad—and tried to ignore the way Karen was making him feel. He wanted to jump right up on the table and shout. It was hard to contain so much happiness.

She gave him another secret smile as she rummaged through the sacks for the plastic knives and forks. He felt like a too-full balloon ready to pop.

He couldn't remember ever being this happy. Not once had he ever imagined that Karen would welcome him into her arms in front of her family. He was here not as a friend, but as her boyfriend.

Boyfriend. Wow, that sounded good.

As one of her sisters brought the barbecued beef and another sister circled around the table, Karen caught his hand and tugged him down beside her on the bench. She didn't let go.

He folded his fingers through hers, her palm small against his. The breeze ruffled her blond locks against his forearm and he breathed in her vanilla scent.

She was like sunrise to his heart. Sitting beside her as she joked with her sisters, he felt overwhelmed by the depth of his feelings.

Karen called out to her grandmother and made a place for her at the table.

"Zach, it's real good to see you here." Helen winked, as if giving him her approval. "Considering Karen's luck with cars, it's just plain common sense for her to be dating a mechanic."

"Gramma, have some iced tea." Color bloomed on Karen's face as she reached for a plastic pitcher, obviously trying to change the subject. "You look like a million dollars in that outfit. Doesn't she look great?"

Mrs. McKaslin's frown deepened. "I don't know what's gotten into you, Mom. You've always had such good common sense."

"I think you look gorgeous, Gramma." Michelle slipped an arm around Helen's slim shoulders. "Except for one thing. You can't wear sneakers with walking shorts. It's a tragedy."

"It is?" Helen looked bewildered. "But Karen helped me."

"Karen knows the basics, but she's no fashion guru or she would have made sure you had a little gold belt and a pair of strappy sandals."

Karen set a cup of iced tea in front of her grandmother. "When we were shopping, we didn't have much time for the shoe department."

"No time for shoes? I can't believe we're related."

So, this is what a real family feels like, Zach thought, watching as Karen's sisters began arguing so loudly over sneakers and sandals, that they drowned out the pastor's first call for attention.

Beside him, Karen bowed her head. The wind ruffled her golden locks against his arm. Looking at her pretty profile, he couldn't get over how lucky he was to be sitting here beside her.

As Pastor Bill began the prayer, Zach bowed his head. Out of the corner of his eye he caught Mrs. McKaslin's gaze. She shook her head at him once, as if she were warning him. As if she were saying he wasn't good enough for her daughter.

The prayer ended. Karen's sisters dove for the bowls of food, chattering again. But the sun didn't feel as bright, even with Karen at his side.

"Honey, are you down here?"

Karen heard her mother's halting step on the stairs

and straightened from the dryer. "Yeah, Mom. What do you need?"

"I couldn't seem to get to sleep. The house is so lonely. It feels empty with most of my girls out on their own."

"You still have Michelle and Kirby. And me." The newly dried towels were hot in her arms as she closed the dryer door with her foot. "Did you take your sleeping pill?"

"I hate taking those—you know that." Mom rounded the corner, easing into sight, wearing an old robe. "You should have left those for tomorrow. It's too late to be doing my laundry."

"When else am I going to do it?" Karen dropped the warm towels on the nearby counter. "Let's get you back upstairs and into bed."

"No, I have too much on my mind."

"A sleeping pill will take care of that."

"I don't want one tonight. What I want to do is talk with my daughter." Mom plucked a towel from the pile. "As long as you have time to talk with your mother."

"I do." Karen kept folding. "What's on your mind? You didn't say much at the picnic. Of course, who could get a word in edgewise with the way Michelle carries on?"

"The picnic is what I want to talk to you about."

Karen took a deep breath. "Okay, I've been waiting for this all day. You might as well get it off your chest."

"It's that Drake boy. I had no idea he would be joining us at the church picnic today."

"Well, he does go to our church."

"Yes, but he didn't have to sit at our table."

"I invited him."

"You should have cleared this with me first."

"What? I haven't done that since high school. I know you don't like Zach, but you don't know him very well."

"Everyone is saying he's your boyfriend."

There was no way she could make this easier for Mom. "Zach *is* my boyfriend."

"That just doesn't sound like you at all, Karen, spending time with a boy like that."

"I'm an adult, Mom. I choose my own friends."

"That Zachary Drake is bound to be a bad influence on you. Normally I would bite my tongue, but I can't do it this time. He doesn't even know who his father is. How can a boy like that grow up to be a decent man?"

"Zach *is* a decent man."

"He's going to take advantage of you."

"What do you mean? He's honest and hardworking." Karen threw down the towel she was folding. "I know you hold grudges, Mom, but to judge other people you hardly know? That's wrong, too."

"You're making a mistake, and it's time you realize it before it's too late. That Drake boy will use you, and then where will you be? For heaven's sake, think about how he's making you behave. Breaking off your engagement, changing your hair, leaving your grandmother to work for you, and that's not all. I know all about your late-night motorcycle ride. Dora Melcher saw you speed by on the way to the river.''

"You think I did something wrong last night." Karen grabbed the laundry basket. "I can't believe this. That's what you think of me? That I'd dishonor myself and my faith?"

Mom said nothing at all.

"Thanks for your confidence." Karen bit back her anger and headed for the stairs.

Mom's not going to change, but I have. She stomped all the way to the second story.

"Michelle?" She rapped her knuckles lightly against the closed door. "Are you up?"

"Yeah" came the muffled response.

Karen set the basket on the floor and turned the knob. The warm glow of a single lamp illuminated both Michelle and Kirby on the floor, playing a game of Scrabble.

"We're living dangerously," Kirby quipped. "Sounds like you might want to join us."

"Did you hear me and Mom?"

Michelle gestured toward the furnace vent. "Every single word. We want to know what you and Zach were doing alone at the river. And why are your dear, loving sisters always the last to hear about the really good stuff?"

Karen knelt on the floor and stole the bowl of buttered popcorn. "Zach was giving me a ride home because my car broke down—"

"*Sure* it did." Michelle winked. "If I was going after Zach, I'd have a breakdown, too."

Karen laughed. What a blessing it was to have sisters. "Okay, I confess. I unhooked the battery cable so he had to help me."

"You did not!" Kirby wasn't fooled. "Is Zach romantic? He seems like the type. He's such a gentleman, even though Mom hates him."

"He is a gentleman, and that's all I'm going to say." Karen's heart filled with the same brilliant warmth she felt when she was with him.

She couldn't wait to see him again.

Zach squinted in the bright morning light, wiped his hands on his jeans and turned the key. The engine rolled over and hummed in perfect tune.

There was no way Karen's car was going to break down now. He'd made a thorough inspection, replaced a belt with a little wear on it and put in a new starter. That ought to hold her until the next tune-up.

Satisfaction filled him as he backed the car into the street. He glanced at the coffee shop. It looked like Karen was in already. A light shone in the back windows, and a trail of water dripped from the front steps into the road.

He pulled into the alley, his pulse hammering with anticipation.

There she was, more beautiful than the morning. In

faded jeans and a short-sleeve sweater, she was busy watering the flowers on the shop's back railing.

Love filled him, gentle and sweet, and he wasn't aware of parking the car. He couldn't look away from her as he crunched across the gravel lot.

"You resuscitated my car." She smiled at him over the bright flowers. "Is that why you're later than usual?"

"Yep. I wanted to change the radiator. Don't want you breaking down again."

"What excellent service. Now I suppose I owe you a cup of coffee."

"That would be a start. We've got to talk about my charges for services rendered." He cradled her chin in his hand. "You owe me ten kisses for all those repairs. I can put it on your bill or collect right here."

"How about in installments?"

"Sure, but I'm going to need a down payment." He kissed her with all the tenderness in his heart. Slowly, to make it last.

When he broke the kiss, she was smiling. There was no mistaking the affection in her eyes, sparkling for the world to see.

Karen McKaslin *liked* him. Maybe she was falling in love with him. He pulled her against his chest and held her tight. She was surprisingly small and fragile. Holding her felt good. It felt right. Cradling her in his arms brought peace to his heart.

The door whispered open.

"Break it up you two. I've got a business to run."

Helen clapped her hands. "I'll finish up the watering. Karen, make this man his coffee and get him on his way. Remember, I don't want any romance to interfere with the running of this shop."

Karen rolled her eyes. "Reverse psychology. Gramma's become an expert."

"I heard that, young lady." Helen stole the hose from Karen. "Go on. And, Zach, I don't want to see any kissing on this premises."

He held the door for Karen. "Then I'll wait until your back's turned."

"You're smarter than you look." Helen winked at him. "So, are there any wedding bells in the future for you two? I think I ought to know, since I am in business with Karen. I don't want her to leave me in a lurch during the honeymoon."

"Gramma! Zach, let's run before she starts in on the great-grandchildren." Karen grabbed him by the wrist and led him inside.

He let the door close, then kissed her again. "Don't worry. Helen isn't looking."

"She's gotten incorrigible. I'd better have Pastor Bill talk to her." Karen leaned back in his arms. "I'll get you a cappuccino. There are oven-hot muffins in the kitchen if you want to help yourself."

"Hey, I like dating the owner. Good perks." He hated letting go of her, but he had to. He couldn't hold her forever. "I see it's another busy morning at the coffee shop."

Karen measured espresso. "Wait until tomorrow. Everyone will be back to school and back to work."

"Then it looks like you'll still be able to get off early?"

"Count on it. Does this mean our competition is still on? You're not backing out?"

"Me? I'm no coward."

"Well, I just thought I should give you a graceful way out."

"You don't have enough faith in my natural athletic abilities. How hard can it be to ride a horse? As far as I can tell, you just sit there."

"This is going to be such an easy victory."

"Victory? No way. Get ready to lose, Karen, because I'm already the winner." He kissed her on the cheek. "I get to spend the afternoon with you."

"Like you said, this can't be hard at all." Karen led Michelle's gelding forward, then stopped to adjust the cinch. "You just climb up and sit there."

"You're mocking me. I can feel it."

"Nope, you said you were a natural athlete. So prove it." She checked the buckle, then gathered the reins. "Mount up."

"Does he bite?"

"Yes." Karen patted Keno's silky neck. "He bucks. He rears. He's a real challenge. I didn't want to give you an easy horse."

"You're kidding. I know you are." His lips grazed

her cheek. "I'm already plotting revenge. Maybe I'll take you mountain climbing for our next date."

"Well, sure, if you're out of the hospital by then."

"Is it too late to ask for mercy?"

"I'm fresh out of mercy, but I do have mints." She handed him a roll of candy. "It'll put Keno in a good mood. Stick your foot in the stirrup. No, the other foot."

"I'm losing my balance."

"Put your hand on the saddle horn. That's it."

Watching him was a sight to behold. He was all muscled control and male grace as he rose up in the saddle and swung his leg over Keno's rump.

"See?" He looked proud of himself. "What did I tell you? I'm a natural."

"We'll see about that." She adjusted the stirrups for him and slipped Keno another mint. The gelding nudged her hand in thanks.

"He's pretty fierce," she teased. "Ready to go?"

"Go? We could stay here. Sitting still is fine by me. I've got a view of the mountains." He gestured toward the rugged Rockies rimming the horizon. "When we get hungry, we're close to home."

"I packed snacks, so there's no reason to hang around here." She hefted the lightweight saddlebag from the fence railing and secured it into place behind her saddle. "Besides, we might want to be alone."

"Without your mother watching from the windows?"

"Watching and scowling." Karen gave Star a peppermint and a gentle pat. "I hope Mom's not making you uncomfortable."

"Well, I do read that 'stay away from my daughter' look loud and clear."

"It's Mom's problem, not yours. She hasn't forgiven me for canceling the wedding. She really wanted Jay for her son-in-law."

"He was good enough for you, being of the respectable Thornton family."

"And about to become a minister." Karen mounted up. "You're twenty times the man Jay is and don't you forget it."

She blushed because she'd spoken without thinking. She couldn't believe she'd exposed her heart like that. And so easily.

But Zach only smiled. "I'm glad you think so. I happen to think you're pretty great, too."

His kiss was a promise, unspoken but deeply felt. A promise that seemed as brilliant as the sun and as real as the earth.

What had Gramma said this morning? *Are there any wedding bells in the future?* As Karen headed Star down the path toward the river, she braced for the same familiar panic she'd associated with the idea of marriage ever since Jay had proposed.

But panic didn't come. Instead, peace filled her, as slow and steady as the wind through the grasses. When she looked into her future, one with Zach at her side, she saw only happiness and laughter.

And love. True love.

She felt it when he reached out to take her hand. They rode side by side, fingers entwined, in silence. They rode toward the river. Keno was used to sharing the trail with Star, and so all Zach had to do was keep in his saddle.

And hold her hand.

Slowly the pasture gave way to low bushes and the path turned onto the public trail that ran the length of the river. Cottonwoods tossed dappled shade over them, and the happy sounds of kids playing rose above the gurgling water.

Karen released Zach's hand and pulled Star to the side of the trail.

Two boys pedaled by on their bikes. "Hi, Zach!" they called.

"Hey, there." He lifted a hand in greeting and suddenly the horse he rode started running.

"Karen. Help!" The saddle rose up to meet him with a slap, tossing him in the air just enough so his seat lost contact with the leather. He grabbed the saddle horn with both hands, tugging back on the one rein he was still holding.

"Whoa, Keno," Karen called out between giggles. "Zach, just pull straight back on the rein. Not hard—"

"It's not working." The ground was a blur. He was slipping to one side and slapping hard against the saddle. The up-and-down motion was hard enough to rattle his teeth. "This is giving me a headache."

"Keno!" Karen was closer now, but not close enough.

Keno skidded down the bank and splashed into the water. Zach tumbled forward, lost contact with the saddle and began to slide. He grabbed the saddle horn with both hands and managed to stay on the horse's back.

"I meant to do that," he called over his shoulder.

The kids watching from the bank howled with laughter, but all he saw were the sparkles dancing in Karen's eyes.

She halted her mare at the water's edge. "Of course, you did. You're a natural. I never doubted it for a minute."

"Thanks for leaving my pride intact." He straightened his Stetson before it tumbled into the river. "Now, how do I turn this beast around?"

"I'll come rescue you." She sent her mare into the water and sidled up to him. "I'm going to have to charge you for this. I hope you're willing to pay my price."

"Depends on what you're charging. Maybe I want to get a couple of other estimates, so I can go with the better deal."

"This *is* the better deal." She brushed a feather-soft kiss on his cheek. "Five kisses. Payable today."

"Wow. That's pretty steep. No payment plan?"

"No. Take it or leave it."

"Then I'd better take it. Five kisses, huh? This must mean that you really like me?"

"You could say that." Tenderness warmed her voice, rare and true.

Karen grabbed Keno's bit and headed for shore. She said nothing more, but she smiled—a little mysterious grin—that told him more than words could ever say.

No one had ever cared for him like this.

His heart soared and gave thanks right where he sat. A whole new future stretched out before him.

As soon as they were alone on the trail, he pulled the horse to a stop and Karen into his arms. "Just so you can't say I'm not a man of my word. Five kisses, like I promised."

He kissed her gently, with all the love in his heart. Tenderly, so she would know. He meant to live every day of his life for her.

Chapter Eleven

The tow truck's headlights slashed through the dark night, casting enough light on the narrow two-lane country road to see the grassy banks.

Zach recognized the crooked signpost that stood forgotten in a spray of dead weeds. A battered mailbox used to perch on that post. It was long gone now, but he could picture it in memory.

Right there in the dirt drive, taken over by grass and wildflowers, he'd waited for the school bus every morning.

He thought about the lost little boy he'd been, in tattered jeans and falling-apart sneakers. How he'd never been able to hold his head up, even when he was that small.

That Drake boy, he'd been called. Sylvia Drake's son. The woman who had three children by three different fathers. Who'd spent days and nights at the local bar, too drunk to make her way home.

Zach pulled the truck to a stop and let the engine idle. He hit the high beams and brightness slashed through the fields. Cows grazed on what was once an unkempt lawn.

All signs of the trailer were gone. Lord knows it had been nearly rusted through when he'd lived there. He tried to shut out the memories of the long nights when hunger gnawed at his stomach. And of the many mornings when his mother made it home, foul smelling and abusive, with one of her endless boyfriends. Zach had felt the sting of their belts more times than he cared to remember.

He'd worked hard to put the chaos of those years behind him. A lot of townspeople still saw that Drake boy in the man he was today, the kid who'd gotten caught stealing to feed his hungry little sister.

In a small town like this, family reputation seemed written in stone. He'd felt that his past would always be a part of him. That no matter how good a man and how honest a businessman, he could never completely wash away the stain of his childhood.

When he was with Karen, she made him a better man. When she looked up at him with affection in her eyes, he felt as if his past didn't matter.

He loved her in a million different ways. He couldn't believe how lucky he was.

God was truly good, to give him Karen's love.

Zach put the truck in gear and drove toward the

lights of town. The night was cloudy; a storm was coming in. Wind whipped the trees and put a chill in the air. Christian country music hummed low on the radio, and the song's lyrics got him to thinking.

Maybe I should propose to Karen. Buy her a ring. Ask her to be my wife.

The thought filled him with joy *and* scared him to death. It was a big step, but he was ready. He had a good job, so he could provide for her, whether or not she wanted to keep her coffee shop. He'd worked hard and saved, so his nest egg was plentiful enough to pay for a new house in town.

Maybe he'd stop by a jewelry store on his next trip to Bozeman. He'd get a ring of gold and diamonds that would look perfect on Karen's hand.

Yes, that's what he'd do.

Zach felt better, at peace, as he drove through the silent town and parked in the dark lot behind his garage.

The wind had a bite to it. Walking through the gravel lot, he shivered. Looked like autumn wasn't far away. He'd better make sure he took Karen hiking in the mountains before colder weather hit.

Halfway up the stairs, he realized he'd forgotten to leave his porch light on. He had the eerie feeling he wasn't alone. The stairs were shadowed, and something at the top moved. A chill snaked down his spine and he didn't know why.

The shadows moved again, and he saw a woman

huddled on the top step, a tattered paper shopping bag beside her. She stood, swaying from side to side.

The strong scent of alcohol fouled the air. Zach stared at the pathetic woman. The shape of her face looked familiar—

Recognition hit him like a pallet of bricks.

This woman was his mother.

"Is that you, boy?" Her voice slurred as if she were heavily drunk. "Don't jus' stand there while your mother's freezin'."

Zach wanted to run. He wanted to pretend this woman didn't exist.

"I haven't seen you in over ten years," he growled. "What do you want?"

"Found myself in Butte the other day and ran into a buddy of mine from here. Maybe you remember him—Chuck Derango. Used to own the Bulldog."

"The only time I went into that place was to drag you home." He stared down at his keys. He didn't know what to do.

A thousand conflicting feelings coursed through him, burning like acid in his gut.

"Chuck said I'd be proud of you. That you've made a real success of yourself. And here I thought you were still working for old Ray Emry." His mother—Sylvia—laughed. "A place like this must make a lot of money."

It all came clear. "That's why you're here. You think you can get even more money out of me."

"I raised you. I ought to get my due."

"We'll see about that." All he wanted to do was hop on his Harley and ride until the cold pain in his chest vanished. He wanted to outrun the sight of this woman and the memories that came with her.

He was a man now, not a boy. He would deal with this problem.

Pushing past her, he unlocked the door and hit the lights. "Come in for now while I make a few calls."

"Nice place you got here." Sylvia ventured in, clutching her shopping bag. She swayed a little, and inside the bag, bottles clanged together.

She sunk into the couch and leaned back. Tufts of short gray hair stuck straight up, and her face was shriveled and yellow tinged. Her aqua slacks and smock were wrinkled and dirty.

"Here." He pushed a soda can into her hand. "Are you hungry?"

"Don't got any Jack Daniel's in that kitchen of yours?"

"You know I don't." It was wrong to hate her— he knew that—but his heart filled with dark, ugly hatred. "I don't want you staying here. I'll find you a room for the night."

Sylvia's eyes gleamed as she studied the apartment. "This place is big enough for you to take in your mama. You could sleep right here on this couch and I'd have a room all to myself."

"You're not welcome here. Ever."

"I could stay here a while." Sylvia acted as if she hadn't heard him. "Maybe get on the wagon for good, once and for all. You must make a lot of money in that shop of yours. Who would have thought a son of mine would be a respectable businessman?''

Zach walked away. He'd let hate into his heart, and he'd never felt so low. He leafed through the Yellow Pages and punched in the local motel's number. No vacancies, the desk clerk explained.

He dialed again, anger roaring through him like a twister, chewing up all his happiness. He tried Bozeman. No rooms there—even at the Y. Full up with holiday travelers.

Now what? There was no way he was spending time under the same roof as this woman. Looking at her brought it all back, the shame and scorn he'd felt as a small, helpless boy. He needed help.

But who could he turn to? Not Karen. There was no way he wanted her to see Sylvia. The last thing he wanted to do was remind Karen of his roots, of what he was deep inside.

And maybe would always be.

There was Pastor Bill, who'd been like a father to him, but he didn't want to trouble the man.

Defeated, Zach hung up the phone. ''You can stay, but only for tonight.''

Sylvia smiled a cat's smile, as if she thought she'd won.

She couldn't be more wrong.

''Come morning, I'll give you a thousand dollars and a ticket on the first bus out of Bozeman. But that's it. If you bother my brother in Bozeman or if you show up here, then I'm cutting you off. Next time you want money, I won't give you a cent.''

She nodded, but her manipulative smile remained.

Pounding on the door startled Zach awake. He bolted upright and the blanket tumbled to the floor. It took him a second to realize he wasn't sleeping in his bed. He was in his living room.

''Zach? You in there?'' It sounded like Dan Drummond, the local sheriff.

Dread shivered through him. He stumbled to the door and yanked it open.

''Got a little problem,'' Dan explained. ''Your mother's passed out on the library steps. Seems she had a private party last night.''

Zach opened his mouth to argue, to say that couldn't be. He'd tried not to sleep too deeply so she couldn't sneak past him. But she'd obviously waited until he'd been in a deep sleep.

''I know this is a sensitive thing, having a mother like that, but I've got her in lockup.''

There was no way news this scandalous would stay a secret. ''How long are you keeping her for?''

''Twenty-four hours. I'll give you a call when it's time to come get her.''

''Thanks, Dan. I appreciate it.'' Zach closed the door and buried his face in his hands.

Alone in the early morning shop, Karen's thoughts kept drifting to Zach as she worked.

I'm too much in love with the man for my own good. I can't even get through the day without wanting to be with him.

The horse ride had been a success. It would take him a long while before he'd be accomplished enough to make Keno behave, but that was all right. They'd had fun riding into the foothills and back to town for ice cream.

Tomorrow, she hoped to take the afternoon off. She and Zach were going hiking.

The rest of my life could be like this, she realized. Happiness filled her, sparkling and true.

She'd never been so at peace. She felt as if everything in her life was in the perfect place, and it had to be. The Lord had led her here. He'd answered her prayers in a way she'd never imagined. She was so thankful.

The door swept open behind her. Was it Zach? She spun around, aching to see him.

Gramma waltzed into the shop. The smile on her face had never been so bright. "Isn't this a fine morning? I can smell autumn in the air."

"You're certainly in a good mood." Karen set the morning's freshly ground espresso next to the machine. "Did you have a good time at your class last night?"

"Did I! It was so informative, but the really good stuff happened before class even started." Gramma tucked her purse under the counter. "Guess what? I have a date for Friday night."

"A date? What about Clyde?"

"What about him? He didn't appreciate the new me, and that's just fine because I found someone who does."

"Who?"

"A very handsome professor of literature. I stopped for an iced tea after the ordeal of the campus bookstore. I was stirring sugar into my tea and he asked to share my table. His name is Willard and he's the nicest man. His birthday is three days before mine. Imagine that!"

"I bet he was blown away by your beauty and wit."

"How did you know?" Gramma chuckled. "I still can't believe it. He's taking me to dinner and the symphony. To think I love classical music, but I've never been able to get anyone to go with me. And now, after all these years, I meet someone who loves Mozart as much as I do."

"Way to go, Gramma. I'm happy for you."

"So am I. Whatever happens, the least I've done is make a friend. What a blessing."

"That explains why you're late," Karen teased as she finished her prep work. "I hope this doesn't get serious. I don't want any romance to interfere with the running of this shop."

"Reverse psychology isn't going to work on me, missy." Gramma collapsed into the nearest chair. "You wouldn't happen to have another pair of shoes with you?"

"What's wrong with the ones you have on?"

"I haven't worn them for twenty minutes and my feet are killing me. I don't care what Michelle says. I'm wearing sneakers every day for the rest of my life."

"That's what you get for listening to anyone who believes beauty comes before comfort." Karen frothed a cup of milk, speaking to be heard over the noisy machine. "I have a pair of sneakers in my car. You're welcome to them."

"I'm not even going to ask what they're doing there."

"I'm used to breaking down and having to walk. What can I say?" Karen poured vanilla flavoring into the bottom of a cup. "You've really changed my life. I have a car I can depend on and a fabulous business partner. Thank you."

"I haven't helped you half as much as you've helped me." Gramma gave Karen a hug. "Is that for me?"

"Yep. We've got customers waiting outside. Go change your shoes while you can. I can handle the shop until you get back."

"You're a dear." Gramma grabbed her latte and Karen's keys from the counter.

Yes, how her life had changed and all for the good, Karen mused as she flipped the sign in the window to Open and unlocked the front door. Several women were already waiting—commuters on their way to work in Bozeman.

It was eight-thirty when Karen looked up again. Gramma carried out a fresh batch of banana muffins, so rich and fragrant that some customers in line groaned at the aroma.

Karen made latte after mocha after cappuccino, chatting with her regulars while Gramma rang up the orders.

Still, there was no sign of Zach. Maybe, when things slowed down, she'd take him a cup of coffee.

The bell on the door jangled, and Gramma's friends crowded in.

"Helen, are those your banana muffins I smell?" Lois led the way up to the counter. "I have to have one of those and your coffee special."

Karen sent Gramma to sit with her friends and whipped up four chocolate-peanut-butter lattes and served them at the table.

"Have you talked with poor Zach this morning?" Lois asked.

"He hasn't been by yet." Karen withdrew a handful of honey packets from her apron pocket.

"I noticed his shop door was closed when I drove by. It's no surprise that poor young man can't show his face." Lois turned grave, shaking her head. "With his mother coming back to town. Drunk. Heard Dan Drummond arrested her and that fellow who's a janitor at the tavern."

"No doubt Zachary's too ashamed to be out and about among us decent folk," Cecilia Thornton commented as she walked into the shop. "I always say that blood shows. I've seen it time and time again."

"That's a terrible thing to say." Karen faced her ex-fiancé's mother. "Zach is a fine man."

"And what about you? You have your mother so upset. What is she going to say when she hears about this?"

"Karen, take a break." Gramma stood. "I'll get Cecilia some coffee and one of my banana muffins."

Karen squeezed her grandmother's hand in thanks. See, it was a doubly good thing she wasn't marrying into the Thornton family.

She headed to the back door and skidded to a stop. Zach was sitting on the bottom step, his face in his hands.

"Zach? Are you okay?" She slipped onto the step beside him.

He shook his head, straightening up.

She'd never seen such sadness on anyone's face. She put her arm around his shoulder. "I heard about your mother coming to town."

"Sounds to me like you heard a lot more than that." He couldn't bear her touch, so good and kind, and bolted from the step. "I've got to get back to the garage."

"Zach, wait." She breezed after him. "Did you want some company? I'd be glad to come over. We could talk."

"I've got work to do."

"You didn't happen to overhear what Cecilia said,

did you? She's not the most compassionate person in town. You can't let her words affect you."

"This has nothing to do with that," he hedged, knowing he wasn't telling the truth. It was wrong, but how could he admit it? How could he say, yes, I heard everything Cecilia said, I opened the door at the right second and it was like hearing my own thoughts.

Karen's touch lit on his forearm. "I care so much about you. This has to be a painful time with your mother back in town."

"I'll be all right." He moved away from her touch again. She was goodness and grace—everything he thought was beautiful and worthy.

"You don't look all right to me." She wouldn't stop caring. "I seem to remember a while ago when I was upset, you sat with me on the step right there. Do you remember what you said?"

He shook his head.

"'You look like someone who needs a friend. Lucky for you, I just happen to be available.'"

"I've got enough friends. See ya." He pushed away from her, the sun in his eyes blinding him. The rush of blood through his ears left him unable to hear anything except the crunch of gravel beneath his boots.

The main street was busy today—just his luck. Maybe if he walked fast, no one would have time to notice him. But he wasn't that lucky. Karen's mom and sister were on their way into the grocery store and Mrs. McKaslin stopped to glare at him.

He knew what she was thinking—not the right kind of man for my daughter.

Heat stained his face, and he stared at the sidewalk and the tips of his boots as he half jogged, half ran to the garage. Sharp whispers rose on the wind.

Shame filled him. With every step he took, he felt the man he'd worked hard to be fall away like a mask.

Maybe that's all it had ever been—just a facade to cover up who he really was inside. An unwanted child born out of wedlock and raised in the shadow of his mother's shame.

The shop phone was ringing, and he let it ring. He couldn't face anything today, not even work. He closed the front bay doors and locked them. The phone fell silent and after a few minutes started ringing again.

Karen. He knew it. It was like her, to take care of people, to check up on him, to make sure he was all right.

Images he'd dared to dream seemed embarrassing now—foolish to think he could propose to Karen and buy her a house. To make a life with her.

The plain and simple truth was that he'd never really had a chance with Karen. He remembered something Helen said. What had she called him? A rebound relationship.

Zachary Drake, you are such a fool.

He hopped on his Harley and headed east, where the sun rose in an endless sky.

* * *

Karen turned off the water faucet, the sprinkler silencing in the thick twilight. Should she try calling Zach again? She'd dropped by his shop twice, only to find it locked and empty. There was no answer at his apartment. She'd left message after message.

He hadn't called.

She was worried about him. He'd been so upset this morning. He'd pushed her away, but she'd refused to take his words seriously.

He's hurting. Maybe he doesn't know how much I really care. It isn't as if I've told him.

She headed inside and picked up the phone. His voice mail answered. There was no sense in leaving another message, so she hung up.

Where was he? Was he with friends? Maybe Pastor Bill? Or was he alone and hurting?

If he doesn't answer the next time I call, I'll drive into town.

That made her feel better, but she couldn't stop shivering. It was as if the night's coolness had settled into her bones.

Chapter Twelve

Seeing Zach lying on a creeper beneath an old pickup inside his shop made Karen's worries fade a little. At least he was okay. He was back to work.

She'd stopped by last night and again early this morning, and he hadn't appeared to be home. He hadn't answered her knock, at least.

Maybe he'd needed space to deal with the sad situation of his mother. It was common knowledge the woman ran off with a man when Zach was only fifteen. Except for yesterday, she'd never been back.

"Hello, handsome," she called out, rattling the paper bag she carried. "You didn't come over, so I brought lunch to you."

He glanced at her from beneath the chrome bumper. "I already ate."

"Then you've got a substantial afternoon snack. I

saved you some of Gramma's potato salad. It was gone before the lunch rush was over.''

"Karen, stop being so nice to me. If I wanted to eat at your shop, I would have gone there." A tool clanged on the cement floor.

"You don't sound all right and you didn't return my calls."

"Busy" came his terse response.

"Are you angry with me? Did I do something to upset you?" She knelt down to peer at him beneath the bumper. "You have to forget what Cecilia Thornton said. She's wrong. I know it. My gramma knows it. And you do, too, right?"

He sighed, dropped his tool with a *clunk* and rolled out from under the vehicle. Grease stained his hands and his shirt. Exhaustion bruised the skin beneath his eyes. He looked terrible, as if he'd been up all night.

Sympathy flooded her. She wanted to hold him until all the pain he had to be hiding faded. She went to him, but he didn't step into her arms. He turned away and hunted for a clean rag to wipe his hands.

"Is your mother still here? I could help you if you needed anything—"

"She's on a bus bound for Phoenix. I'm praying she stays on it." He kept his back to her as he wiped the grease from his hands.

His shoulders looked slightly hunched, and she didn't doubt he was hurting.

She should tell him he's not alone and say the words she longed to—*I love you.* She should take the risk and tell him how cherished he was. To her. As the one man she wanted to love for the rest of her life.

Just do it. She took a step toward him. "Zach, I—"

"Look, I don't have time right now. I've got to get this finished." Zach tossed down the rag, his shoulders dipping more. "Thanks for the lunch. Next time, wait until I come to the shop, okay?"

Karen stared, unbelieving, as he held out a five-dollar bill. "What's going on? You don't have to pay. I—"

"Take the money." He shoved it into her hand. "See you."

She stared at the money, creased and worn. What was happening? "Zach, would you listen? I want to tell you how I feel—"

"Summer's over, and I've got to get back to work." He rummaged through his toolbox. "Maybe you can find someone else to help you get over Jay. I'm no longer the man to do it."

"But—" Tears burned in her throat. "What about all those kisses?"

"They were nice. No strings attached, right?" He found the tool and gripped it, white-knuckled, in his hand. "I don't want to hurt your feelings, Karen, but did you really think anything could work out between us? I live above a garage. I've got a family reputation that would put yours to shame. Cecilia Thornton is right. Your mother doesn't want me around you."

"But they're wrong. You're gentle and intelligent and kind, and I—"

"I don't want to see you again." The words tore him apart, and he said them as quietly as he could. It was for her own good, even if she couldn't see that.

All those sweet kisses had come to this. It tore him up watching the tears fill her eyes, but then she blinked them away.

Her chin shot up. "I'm not a fair-weather friend, and I thought there was more to you than this. We had a good time together. I thought—"

"That's all we had. A good time." He cut her off, turned his back, afraid she'd say the words that would make him start to believe again. Believe in what could never be. "I know you're thinking this is about my mother coming to town and what Cecilia said, but you're wrong. You're too nice for me."

"I see." Her words sounded stilted, without emotion. She looked shell-shocked.

"I don't want to hurt you, Karen, so maybe it would be better if we didn't see each other again."

She fell silent.

He doubted she knew just how much she meant to him. There was nothing more to say, so he stretched out on the creeper and scooted back under the pickup.

Safely hidden, he released a deep breath. Sylvia Drake's son had no business loving a woman like Karen McKaslin.

He watched her walk away. Her slim ankles and

dainty white sneakers whispered across the cement floor and then out of sight.

His heart broke in a million sharp pieces.

Zach knew as sure as the sun was in the sky that Karen was out of his reach.

And always would be.

You're too nice for me. Zach's words rang like a bell, over and over in Karen's mind. Somehow she made it down the street, the sidewalk a blur at her feet, the storefronts hazing together. She choked out a hello to Nora Greenley who was waiting at the curb while a box boy loaded groceries into the trunk of her car.

Karen stumbled up the steps of the coffee shop, passing by the flower boxes that smelled sweet like summer.

Summer's over, and I've got to get back to work, Zach had said.

Is that all it was? A good time?

The bell clamored in the nearly empty shop. A group of women sat in the sunny corner, devotionals and Bibles stacked in front of them. Thankfully, they were busy and didn't notice her. Karen turned her head anyway. She didn't want anyone to see the tears in her eyes.

At least he was honest with me, she thought. At least Zach wanted nothing but a good time, a few motorcycle rides and a fishing trip.

But that didn't seem like the truth or keep her heart from rending.

Be calm, she told herself, blinking back tears. She wasn't about to let anyone see her so sad and wonder why.

She grabbed her purse and keys from under the counter as Gramma shouldered through the kitchen doors.

"Good, I'm glad to see you're ready to go. Did Zach like my potato salad?"

"You know he does." Karen kissed her grandmother's cheek. "I'm off. The rest of the afternoon should be quiet."

"I can handle it. I *am* a businesswoman."

"And an excellent one. Look how successful the shop has become. I'll open up early tomorrow, so don't bother to come in until late."

"Maybe that's not a good idea." Gramma followed her to the back door. "You look pale and your eyes are glassy. Are you ill?"

"Just tired." Which was the truth. "I've got to go."

"You have a fun time with your handsome young man."

Karen couldn't answer. Zach wasn't hers. He never had been. She closed the door and dashed down the stairs, the pain inside her hurting more with each step she took.

How could she have been so foolish? No man was ever going to love her deeply. She was too ordinary, too dependable. True love didn't happen to girls like her.

She settled behind the steering wheel and turned the ignition. The old Ford coughed to a start—hadn't Zach promised her that this car was in good shape?— and she headed into the alley. The street through town was quiet, but it took her past Zach's garage.

What had he said about her kisses? They were nice. Lukewarm.

Dear Lord, I thought he was the one. She swiped wetness from her cheeks. *I loved him, and I thought he loved me.*

How could she have been wrong?

Dust lifted behind her on the driveway and clouded the air when she parked the car in front of the garage at home. The sun was hot, but the wind was definitely cooler.

Zach was right. Summer *was* over. No more fishing trips or rides along the river. No more kisses beneath a star-filled sky.

"Karen!" Mom called from the front steps. "Are you going to be home for dinner? I feel up to cooking. You aren't going out with that Drake boy again, are you?"

"No, Mom."

"That's my sensible girl. Supper's at six sharp. See you then."

Sensible girl. The words pierced Karen's soul and stayed there like a barbed wire hooked firm, words that made her feel less than valuable. She'd colored her hair, changed her life, but had it made any difference?

Sensible, plain and responsible. Was that all Zach saw in her? He'd had fun, he said, but he'd only been helping her get over Jay. That's what he'd said. Part of her didn't believe him—or couldn't.

I want someone to love me, Lord. Is that too much to ask? I don't want to be alone the rest of my life.

But she didn't want to settle, either. She didn't want a lukewarm marriage.

What was God's plan for her? She didn't know.

Star nickered from the far end of the corral and trotted over. Karen grabbed the lead rope looped around a fence post and snapped it onto the mare's halter.

"We're going for a run, girl." Karen crawled through the fence rails and mounted. Her horse was something a girl could always count on.

They loped through the fields toward the river trail. Karen squeezed all thoughts of Zach from her mind.

Maybe there was no such thing as true love. It was only a fairy tale, and nothing more.

She wanted the Lord to guide her, to show her the answers for sure. She felt so very lost.

So alone.

Zach looked up, recognizing the sound of the engine—Karen's car. The morning was calm and almost cool, and she drove past with her windows up. He could hardly see her through the sheen on the glass.

Stop thinking about her. There's no point in dwelling on what was past. Aching tenderness cut like a blade through his chest, and he turned his attention back to the engine he was in the middle of rebuilding.

His relationship with Karen was over. He didn't like it. He'd give anything to have the right to marry her.

But last night, prayer had put everything in perspective. He had to trust God's will for his life. He had to believe that everything happened for a greater reason—and there were some things a man couldn't have. That's all there was to it.

This morning, he planned to buy his coffee from the diner and stay away from Karen McKaslin.

"What is with this car?" In the parking lot behind her shop, Karen gave the tire a kick. Steam was wafting from beneath the hood and the temperature gauge had been climbing all the way into town.

"I'm going to find another mechanic." She wasn't about to ask Zachary Drake to repair her car again. Especially since he'd been doing a lousy job.

"Morning, Karen!" Jodi called out as she cut across the alley. "Your car is smoking."

"I know. I have bad car luck." Karen slung her purse over her shoulder and hurried up the stairs. She was late, and she was opening the shop alone. This morning Gramma had a meeting at the church.

Karen was unlocking the door when she heard a car pull into the lot. For a second she thought it was

Zach come for his early-morning coffee. Then she remembered he said that he didn't want to see her again.

Gramma parked her snazzy car, climbed out and shut the door. "Surprised to see me, aren't you? I woke up before the alarm and the house seemed lonely. I figured if I showed up here, I could sweet-talk my granddaughter into making me a cup of coffee."

"You've got that look in your eye." Karen wasn't fooled as she held the door. "Why are you really here?"

"Nothing." Gramma appeared perfectly innocent as she dropped her purse and keys on the counter. "I happened to notice yesterday that Zach was in his garage working all afternoon. When he was supposed to be on a date with you."

"No, I'm not going to talk about that." Karen headed straight for the kitchen.

"Did you two have a disagreement?"

"Not a disagreement. I wouldn't call it that." Karen yanked open the freezer and grabbed the heavy bag of coffee beans. "That's all I'm going to say."

"Fine. All right. I respect your privacy." Gramma took the bag from Karen's arms. "Let me do the grinding. You don't look like you slept a wink last night."

"It's your morning off." Karen regained possession of the bag. "Sit down, put up your feet and relax. I'll have your latte ready in a few minutes."

"If that's what you want." Gramma went around the dining room, opening the curtains and tying them back.

Sunlight washed into the room. It felt like any other day. The sun rose and soon people would be hurrying to work and taking their children to school.

When Karen felt as if her life would never be the same. How could it be? She'd lost her dreams of Zach. She'd lost his friendship, too.

By the time she finished Gramma's latte, she found her grandmother in the kitchen, whipping up muffins.

"Just set it there on the counter, dear," Gramma said as she filled the tins. "Are you ready to tell me what happened?"

"No." Karen reached for the mixing bowl and rinsed it in the sink. "Oh, all right. I'll tell you. All this time I thought Zach…well, it turns out that he's not interested in me."

"That's nonsense. I've got eyes. I can see that boy's in love."

"No. He said he was just having fun."

"That sounds ridiculous." Gramma slipped the tins into the oven. "I was married for a long time, and you learn to break the code. Seems to me that this happened after his mother's arrest. Maybe he thinks he has something to be ashamed about."

"Nice try, but you don't want to admit your granddaughter is plain and unexciting. I spend my days making coffee and helping my sisters look after my mom."

"Maybe he figures he'd reject you before you reject him."

"Maybe, but he thinks I'm too nice. That's the problem." Karen dried off the bowl and fit it into place in the mixer. "It isn't because of his mother. He told me that."

"That man's protecting his heart, if you want my opinion." Gramma set down the oven mitt and wrapped Karen in a hug. "Zach has never had a real family. He's never known what it's like to have unconditional love. The kind that can never be broken. Maybe God sent you into his life for a reason. To teach him that."

"Nice try, Gramma, but I don't think so."

"Talk to him. Find a reason to go to his shop and try to make him listen. I've seen how happy you two are together. A love like that is worth fighting for."

"Even if it's one-sided?" She was afraid to believe otherwise. "He said—"

"People say lots of things to protect their hearts. Now trust your grandmother, make him some coffee and go talk to the boy."

"I can't." Karen turned to the flour canister and started measuring.

"Hey, Zach." Tommy Clemmins rode his bike into the garage, his book bag dangling over one handlebar. "My tire's flat again. I guess I rode over a nail."

"I guess." Zach grabbed a rag, left his work, and knelt down to take a look. "I'd better patch that. Why don't you grab an apple juice from the refrigerator over there? I have a box of chocolate doughnuts on my toolbox.''

''Thanks!'' Tommy dropped his books on the floor.

Zach grabbed his glue gun and a patch from his bottom drawer and went to work. Before Tommy was finished with his second doughnut, the tire was holding air.

''I'm not even gonna be late to school! Thanks, Zach.'' Tommy hopped on his bike and rode out of sight.

Forgetting his book bag.

That kid. Shaking his head, Zach grabbed the bag and jogged outside. Tommy biked back across the street in a wide space between a school bus going one way and a car going the other.

''I know, I know. I'm gonna be in big trouble if I forget my homework one more time.'' Tommy skidded to a stop and looped the book bag over his handlebar.

He pedaled into the street, looking over his shoulder to wave.

Zach saw it all in a flash. The loaded hay truck ambling down the road, the surprise on the driver's face, Tommy turning to stare at the oncoming truck and realizing he was in danger. The boy froze with fear.

The semi's brakes squealed, locking up. There was no way the driver could stop in time. Zach was already running. He grabbed Tommy by the shoulders and hurled him toward the sidewalk. The semi's grill slammed into Zach's shoulder and back, tossing him into the air.

Zach didn't feel anything—not pain or fear. He hit the asphalt but he couldn't feel that, either. It was as if it were happening to someone else. He rolled to a stop on his side, his forehead resting against the cool cement curb.

"My stars!" The Mint Mocha Special Gramma was serving slipped from her hand and clattered to the floor. "Tell me that isn't Zachary Drake."

Through the windows, Karen saw a loaded hay truck jackknifing in the middle of town, brakes squealing. A bicycle flew into the air and slammed against the brick front of John Corey's hardware store. A little boy lay sprawled on the sidewalk, then climbed to his feet.

"It isn't Zachary Drake." Marj Whitly leaned in her chair for a better look. "It's that little Clemmins boy. He's getting up. He's fine. What a close call!"

Karen left the espresso machine, coffee dripping, and raced around the counter. Sure enough, the little boy looked fine.

Then why was the fire chief racing out of his store, shouting orders at everyone in sight? He ran past the boy and knelt in the street. Karen recognized the grease-stained work boots just visible behind the motionless semi.

She was out the door before she even realized she

was running. Sprinting across the street and pushing around people gathering in a knot on the sidewalk.

"Stay back, everyone, let them work." The sheriff caught Karen by the arm and held her. "You have to give them room, Karen."

She could only stare in horror at how motionless Zach looked. Broken and lifeless, as if he weren't even breathing.

"He's going to be okay," the lawman told her, not letting go of her. "Someone take her. Nora, is that you? Take her back to her grandmother. She can't do any good here."

"No." She was only vaguely aware of Nora Greenley, her grandmother's friend, taking her by the hand. Terror made her cold as she watched one of the town doctors stop his car and race across the road.

The little boy was crying as one of the town's volunteer firemen looked at his bruised arm. "Zach's gonna die and it's all my fault."

"He's not going to die," the fireman reassured him.

Karen could see Zach was breathing. His chest rose and fell, shallow and rapid. He looked ashen, and a streak of blood trickled down his face from a cut on his forehead.

He looked like he could die.

Someone had grabbed the backboard from the fire hall around the corner, and four men gingerly strapped Zach to it.

The men were busy setting up an IV, and Karen

was hardly aware of her grandmother taking her hand. The medical helicopter arrived, landing in a field on the other side of the railroad tracks.

"Probable broken vertebrae," John Corey called above the beat of the chopper's blades. "He's alert but in a lot of pain."

"He'll be okay." Gramma sounded sure of it. "What he needs are extra prayers and loved ones around him. Come, I'd better drive you to the hospital."

But he doesn't love me, Karen almost said, but watching four men lift Zach on the backboard and carry him across the street, kept her silent.

No, he hadn't said he didn't love her. He hadn't looked at her the whole time he'd been rejecting her, as if he hadn't been telling the truth.

She was afraid to believe it, but maybe Gramma was right. *Zach is as afraid of being rejected as I am.*

She didn't know if it were true or not, but it was worth finding out. Having Zach's love was worth risking her heart.

"Please take me to the hospital," she asked her grandmother. "I'm too upset to drive."

"Knew you'd see things my way. Nora promised she'd lock up, so let's get going." Gramma slipped an arm around her shoulder.

The helicopter took off with an ear-ringing racket. Karen watched it. Zach was in there, on his way to the emergency room. *Please, Lord, take good care of that man. I love him.*

Chapter Thirteen

There were one hundred and six ceiling tiles on his side of the hospital room. Zach closed his eyes, and all he saw behind his lids were images of the ceiling tiles.

The surgery to fuse vertebrae in his neck had gone well, and they'd moved him out of ICU after the first day. He'd been trapped in this tiny room for three days and already he was going stir-crazy.

Strapped to the bed in traction, he couldn't turn his head to see the window. Somewhere out there the sky was blue. There were cars to fix, trails to ride and mountains to climb.

What had the doctors said? His chances of walking again were fifty-fifty.

Lord, I have to get out of this room. Please.

"Good to see you're awake." Pastor Bill appeared beside the bed, his face pale with fatigue and worry.

"I sent your sister home. She stayed the night by your bed again. You should know there's someone who's been waiting for you to feel well enough for a visit. I'll be waiting outside."

"I don't want any visitors—" But Pastor Bill was gone.

"Hi, Zach." Karen appeared, carrying a vase of cheerful yellow flowers. "Let me put these where you can see them."

The harsh words he'd said to her haunted him, and he wished he could vanish. He'd done what he had to do. There was no way he was the right man for her.

She disappeared, her sneakers slightly squeaking on the floor. Zach heard a thud and a clink and the flowers appeared, propped on the windowsill.

She returned to his bedside, avoiding his gaze. He couldn't stop the shame creeping through him, leaving him feeling small. If he hadn't pushed her away, she would be reaching for his hand right now. Gazing at him with that sparkling affection in her eyes. Saying something to make him feel better.

He loved her with all the depth of his soul, whether it was right or wrong. He'd been tough on her, and here she was, a friend once more, bearing flowers and well wishes.

"Gramma sends her best. You know what she said?"

He didn't answer.

"That you'd be up and walking in no time. She'll sneak you in some of her taco cheese and macaroni casserole when she gets the chance."

Zach stared at the off-white ceiling tiles. A polite exchange—that's what she intended. He missed her smile and her gentle teasing. He wished he could take her hand and have the right to hold on to her.

She approached the bed. "Is there anything I can do for you?"

"Not a thing."

"I could read to you."

What he needed was her. Zach closed his eyes and tried to ignore the pain the medication couldn't kill. As bad as he hurt, it was nothing compared to the pain in his heart. If only he had the right to make her his.

"Is your pain worse? I'll get the nurse—"

"I don't need the nurse. Seeing you—" Makes me love you even more. He couldn't tell her. It wouldn't be right. There were some things a man couldn't have.

"Maybe I should let you rest. I'll be out in the waiting room in case you need anything."

"What do you mean? You're staying?"

"Do you think I'd leave you when you're hurt?" Karen's chin lifted, and he'd never seen this side of her. "I think you might not have been honest with me in your shop. You spent a lot of time telling me to leave and why, but I know how it felt when you kissed me."

"I don't think you should be here."

"But I love you." She crossed her arms over her chest as if she were protecting herself. "Do you know that? Couldn't you feel that, too?"

"You love me?" The medication must be messing with his mind. There was no way Karen genuinely, unconditionally loved a man like him.

He might want it more than anything, but it was impossible.

Her bottom lip trembled. "I know what you said before, about summer being over and I'm too nice for you, but I'm not sure that's what you really feel. Didn't we have something special? I thought we were falling in love, and then I'm not certain what happened."

"I thought it was obvious. I'm not the man for you."

"I think you are." Couldn't he see that she was risking her whole heart? "I don't care who your mother is or if she might come back to town one day. Do you think I do? Is that why you broke things off?"

"We can't be together. It wouldn't last."

"Why not? Don't you know I only see the good in you? There's a lot of good."

"I'm no one special, Karen."

"To me, you are. I see the hero in you, in an ordinary man with an ordinary life. I love you. I want to marry you and have a family with you. When I look at you, I see a courageous and gentle man I can trust with my heart."

"I'd give anything to be that man, but I'm not."

"You are to me. Or am I the problem? You said I was too nice for you. I thought you could see something good and special inside me. Tell me that you do, please. Even just a little."

How could he tell her that he saw more—much more? She'd awakened his heart. Her quiet beauty was more lovely to him than any in the world.

He loved her more than he thought possible. If only he could change his past and who he was....

It felt written in stone.

"I don't want you here." The words sounded harsh when he didn't mean them to be. He just wanted to spare his heart.

"You didn't answer my question. But either way, that's an answer, too." Her bottom lip trembled. "I guess this is goodbye."

She walked away, just like that, taking his heart with her.

Footsteps tapped into the room, and Zach realized he wasn't alone.

"That was some show," Pastor Bill commented. "I tried to stay out in the hall to give you two some privacy, but I couldn't help overhearing. Why did you send that woman away? The one who loves you even if you might not walk again?"

"What I had with Karen is over."

"Why's that? Because you're strung up in this hospital room while your back heals?"

"We both know I'm not the kind of man Karen McKaslin is going to marry and I never will be." Zach was exhausted and wrung-out. Burning, grinding pain radiated up his spine. He'd lost Karen forever.

"You know what the Bible says," Pastor Bill began thoughtfully. "'...*Those who become Christians become new persons. They are not the same anymore, for the old life is gone. A new life has begun.*'"

"That doesn't mean—"

"It does. The past is erased, and it would be foolish to throw away the future because of it. God wants good things for you, Zachary Drake. Believe that."

How could he? How could it be true? It didn't feel true. Zach closed his eyes, overwhelmed, thinking about what the pastor had said.

"What are you doing back?" Gramma looked up from serving her friends a round of steaming mochas. "I told you, running this place without you isn't a burden. I've got Michelle coming in an hour to help me close up."

Karen dropped her keys on the counter. "I'll do it."

She was so angry with Zachary Drake! She'd laid her heart open and told him how she truly felt. Thinking it would make a difference. For him. For his recovery. Especially for their future.

And he hadn't done the same. He hadn't told her how he felt. He hadn't said the words that mattered. Maybe he never loved her at all. Not even a little bit.

She was still so incredibly angry with him! No one—not even Jay—had ever made her this angry. She punched through the kitchen doors and turned on the faucet. Hot water steamed into the sink and she began rinsing dishes, then stacking a load of mugs into the dishwasher.

He's all that matters to me, she realized. He's still all I care about.

The door whispered open behind her. "What happened at the hospital? Is Zach all right?"

"His recovery is going well, if that's what you mean." A plate slipped from her fingers and crashed into the sink. "He's looking forward to your visit."

Gramma sidled up to the counter. "I thought you were going to stay at his side until he's out of the hospital."

"He told me to go." Karen retrieved the plate and it slipped from her fingers again. "He doesn't want me to come back."

"That doesn't sound right. I don't think he's telling the truth. He's injured, and it can't be easy worrying if he'll walk again. Maybe he's saying that because he feels he has to."

"There's nothing more I can do." Karen left the plate in the sink and shut off the water. "I'm through with Zachary Drake."

She'd survived other breakups just fine. She'd get over this one, too.

Except this time it was Zach. Zach, the man who made her laugh, who made her feel unique and treasured.

It wasn't going to be easy getting over him. If she ever could.

Chapter Fourteen

"I had such a wonderful time at the symphony," Gramma mused as she wiped down the coffee shop's counter. "Willard and I had coffee and dessert afterward and talked until one in the morning."

"I'm glad you like him." Karen squeezed water from the mop. "Are you two going out again?"

"Next weekend we're taking in a Shakespearean play. Just when I'd given up finding someone like Willard, he walks into my life. Imagine that. He could be the one."

"I hope so." Karen mopped the floor, happy for her grandmother. It was only the beginning of her relationship with the professor, but maybe he would end up being the love of Gramma's life.

Karen hoped so. She wanted to think true love existed in this world and happened to women like her.

The phone rang, and Gramma was closest to it.

Karen swiped the mop across the wood floor, then dunked it into the soapy bucket.

"Zachary Drake! What are you doing calling here? How's the hospital treating you? Terrible food, is that right? I did plan to visit you this week. I'll come with my casserole, promise." Gramma laughed. "Karen, it's for you."

Karen stared at the receiver her grandmother held out for her. Twice she'd risked her heart; twice she'd tried to tell Zach that she loved him.

She'd been hurt enough. She'd risked everything for him, and she wasn't about to do it again.

Gramma waggled the receiver. "Go on," she whispered. "He wants to talk to you."

"Tell him I'm busy." She went back to her mopping.

"Zach, Karen's being stubborn and she won't come to the phone. Don't worry, I have a way of convincing her to do anything—"

Gramma meant well, but she should understand. If Zach believed he wasn't the man for her. If he didn't want her, then there was nothing she could do.

Not one thing.

She marched out the door and stayed outside until Gramma hung up the phone.

"Look at all these flowers," Chief Corey commented when he walked into Zach's hospital room. "It looks like a florist shop in here. How does it feel to be the town hero?"

"I'm no hero."

"Yeah? Well, that's not what everyone's saying. You saved Tommy's life, and no one's going to forget that. You're going to be the most popular man in town. Of course, you don't need throngs of women adoring you. You're dating Karen McKaslin."

"We're friends, that's all."

"Are you kidding? She's in love with you."

I know. Zach remembered how she'd stood where John was standing now, saying she loved him.

A knock sounded at the door. Helen and three of her friends waltzed into the room, bearing fantastic-smelling food and colorful balloons.

"How's our town hero?" Mabel Clemmins, Tommy's grandmother, asked.

"Town hero," John repeated, reaching for his hat. "Get used to it. You're going to hear it a lot."

After his visitors left and as the evening wore on, Zach caught himself missing Karen. And thinking about what Pastor Bill had said.

He could have been killed when he'd thrown himself in front of the hay truck. No doubt about it. The doctors had told him he was lucky. Already he could wiggle his toes.

It was time for him to let the past rest. He'd stopped being Sylvia Drake's son long ago. Pastor Bill was more of a parent to him than his mother ever was.

He was his own man. He raised his brother and sister, ran his own business and had many good friends in his hometown. If God had spared his life for a reason, then Zach knew why.

He'd been put on this earth to love Karen Mc-Kaslin. And a gift like that was too precious to waste.

"C'mon, Karen, he's called like every day this week." Michelle hung up the phone. "You're going to drive that hunk away."

"I don't know why he's calling me."

"I wonder. He's only the most popular guy in town. A real hero. Everyone says so. Why he wants to talk to you is a mystery, but he keeps calling. You should at least be polite and talk to him."

"I've said more than enough. If I humiliate myself one more time in front of him, I'm going to lie down and never move again." Karen rolled the dice and moved her Monopoly piece onto Vermont Avenue.

"Ooh! You owe me," Kirby announced across the kitchen table.

Whatever Zach had to say to her, it didn't matter. Karen handed play money to her sister. She was through risking her heart on Zachary Drake.

Now, if only she could stop being in love with him. Because she *was* in love with him. She knew she always would be.

Three weeks later, Zach set the walker against the garage wall. He'd had enough of that contraption. What he wanted was to see Karen, but she hadn't been in the shop. Running errands, Helen had explained. A real excuse, this time.

His homecoming had been great. Pastor Bill had insisted he stay with his family until he was stronger, and Zach had accepted. The well wishes hadn't stopped.

If Zach needed proof of what Bill had said, about being made new, then he had it. He'd been the one who let his past affect him. When he looked at himself more kindly, he might not see himself as a hero, but he did see an average guy who'd been about as dumb as they came.

He'd hurt Karen. He'd pushed her away. Truth be told, her love scared him. But true love, he was learning, wasn't something that could ever fade. She still loved him—or so Helen and Karen's sisters assured him.

How did he get her back?

He opened his toolbox and went to work. His back hurt, but it felt good to be busy. The ring he'd bought today weighed heavily on his thoughts—a sparkling solitaire on a gold band. The one he planned to give her when she agreed to marry him.

Like that would be an easy question to ask her.

The next time you see her, just take her by the hand, bend down on one knee and say the words.

He figured it sounded a lot easier than it was, but he'd find the courage. Because he loved her.

"Hey, Zach," John called from next door where he was sweeping his sidewalk. "Guess who's coming this way with her bank deposit? Just thought you'd like to know.''

Zach wiped his hands on a rag. Okay, you can do it. Just give her that grin she likes and don't take no for an answer.

Armed with courage, he headed out the door.

Karen saw him immediately. Her eyes widened and her jaw dropped. She must not have realized he was in his garage.

''Hi,'' he called out, but before he could say anything more, she slipped between the buildings and walked out of sight.

''Proof that she isn't over you,'' John commented, broom in hand. ''Trust me, I'm an expert when it comes to romance.''

Zach waited, watching for her to reappear farther down the street. Yep, there she was, emerging from the side street near the bank.

His heart ached at the sight of her. He wasn't afraid, not anymore, because he knew he was the only man for her. One day soon, he was going to make her believe it.

It had been a tough week, and Karen was glad she had the afternoon off. She grabbed her denim jacket from the coat tree at the front door of her shop. ''Michelle, don't scare off the customers. Gramma and I are trying to actually make a profit this month.''

''Ha ha. Don't lose track of time. We meet at Gramma's house at six sharp. We've got to make sure our grandmother is smartly dressed for the upcoming winter season. I was thinking she needs some of those stylish new boots.''

''I can see this is going to be an ordeal,'' Karen teased. ''I never should have invited you along.''

''Face it, Gramma needs my expert fashion sense.'' Michelle grabbed the mop and wrung it out in the bucket. ''You could use some help too, Karen.''

''I can finally afford a few new things, but I'm scared to trust you. Last time I did, you turned my hair green.''

''You know what I think? Leopard skin and leather. I bet we could make a whole new look for you.''

''Stop teasing!'' Karen balanced her dish of soft ice cream with one hand and opened the front door with the other.

The crisp air of autumn smelled earthy and rich. Dried leaves skidded down the street, and kids just released from school ran down the sidewalk screaming and laughing.

''Butterscotch sundae, just for you, Star.'' Karen leaned against her horse's flank, where the animal stood obediently in a parking spot off the main street.

It was too cold to eat ice cream, but it brought back the sweetest memories. Of her and Allison as little girls, always to be found on their horses. Sharing candy and snacks, laughing and carefree.

There were more memories to make in her life, and Karen wondered what they would be.

A car slid into the parking space beside her—a polished red convertible. A classically dressed, handsome older woman emerged from the vehicle. "Why, if it isn't my beautiful granddaughter."

"Hi, Gramma. You're looking radiant."

"Being in love will do that to a woman. Willard took me out to lunch and a movie. I haven't had so much fun in ages. He's coming to church on Sunday, so help me prepare your mother. She's not likely to approve of me dating."

"She's bound to like him." Karen gave her grandmother a hug. "He's a nice man. I think he's perfect for you."

"Me, too. I'll see you this evening. I can't wait to go shopping. I need the right dress to wear on my date Saturday night."

"We'll find something to make you look gorgeous," Karen promised.

Gramma hurried up the stairs and out of the wind, her step had never been so lively—ever since she'd been dating her distinguished English professor.

And here I thought true love didn't happen to women like us.

But she'd been wrong. While she was happy for her grandmother, Karen wouldn't mind finding that for herself. No—she wasn't going to even think about Zach.

Star nudged her hand, eager for more ice cream, and she gave the horse a big spoonful.

A yellow car slipped into the parking spot on the

other side of Star. The door opened and a man emerged, dressed in a T-shirt and jeans. Karen recognized the cut of his handsome profile and the dark shock of untamed hair tumbling over his forehead.

"Zach." She couldn't believe it was him. How had he sneaked up on her?

"Hi, Karen." Zach closed the car door and leaned against it, slipping his hands in his pockets. "You're looking good."

"You look better than I saw you last." What she needed to do was leave quickly, before he could see that she still loved him. She inched away.

"They say I'll be almost as good as new, but I have to take it easy for a while."

She took two more steps back. A few more, and she could dart up the steps. Could he tell by looking at her that she was still in love with him? Embarrassed, she searched for something polite to say. "I'm glad you're walking. You gave all of us a real scare."

"God's been very good to me. I'm pretty happy to be up on my feet." He rubbed his brow, looking troubled. "I was rude to you in the hospital, and I'm sorry."

"Don't mention it. I was wrong to push myself on you like that. Especially when you were so hurt."

"Why don't you stop trying to run away, come over here and let me apologize properly? It's the least I can do after the way I behaved."

"You don't have to apologize. Really." It's not like an apology could change the truth.

"I need to tell you how sorry I am. I said things I wish I hadn't."

"And I was wrong." It hurt to think how foolish she'd been, risking her heart. She changed the subject. "I'm glad you're back to work."

"Not officially. I've been tinkering for a few hours a day to keep busy." He gestured to the Chevy gleaming like new. "See what I did to your old car."

"That can't be the rusted-out rattletrap I used to drive."

"One in the same."

She ran her fingers over the dent-free front left fender. The crack in the windshield was gone. The dings and dents and rust patches had disappeared. "The paint looks great."

"That was her original color. Look." He opened the door so she could see the interior. "I finished the upholstery this morning. It's like it was when she was new."

"How did you do this? I'd never know it was the same vehicle."

"All it took was a little work." Zach didn't tell her how he'd thought about what Pastor Bill had said to him. How being made new meant his past didn't have to influence his future. "I figured we all deserve a second chance, even a car."

"You can make a lot of money selling her now."

"Got a buyer all lined up. A collector who's happy to have it. He's coming for it this weekend."

"I'm glad."

Good, she'd managed to keep it impersonal. But it was time to go. The last thing she wanted to do was talk about Zach's future, a future they wouldn't share together. "Good luck to you. I'll see you later—"

"Wait. I'm thinking of buying a new house in the new subdivision here in town. What do you think?"

Why was he asking her about a house? Her foot hesitated on the bottom step. "A house is always a good investment."

"It's also a pretty smart way to start a marriage."

A marriage? Did she hear him right? Why was he saying this to her? She couldn't afford to hope, not anymore. She ran up the steps.

"Karen, wait!"

For what? For him to say she was a sensible woman to marry, now that he'd thought about it. She pushed through the front doors and the bell overhead jangled violently.

Customers turned in their chairs to stare at her. Michelle peered over the top of the cash register. Karen kept her head down and headed straight through the dining room.

The bell jingled behind her—it had to be Zach. Why was he doing this to her? Why couldn't he go find some other nice woman and settle for her?

Out of breath, Karen shouldered through the back door and onto the walkway behind the coffee shop. Maybe Zach would get sidetracked in the dining room and she'd be free of him.

The door squeaked open behind her. No such luck.

"Hey, Karen. Wait up. You're really making me work for this. I've got this pain shooting down my leg. I can't keep running, okay?"

"Then stop following me." She'd humiliated herself enough.

"What choice do I have?" He limped up to her, breathing heavily. "I've tried calling you. I've tried talking to you, but you won't stay around long enough for me to tell you how I feel."

"Zach, I can't—"

"I don't want to lose you."

She felt as if her heart were breaking all over again. "No, we can't be friends. Acquaintances, maybe, in time—"

Something glinting in the sun caught her eye—a diamond ring. Zach was holding a diamond ring.

"I wanted to show you this." He took her hand tenderly. "Do you like it?"

The diamond was pure white and oval shaped, ringed with emeralds. "It looks like an engagement ring."

"That's because it is."

He knelt down in front of her, still holding her hand.

What was he doing? He *couldn't* be about to propose. Not after what had happened. "I can't marry you. You know that."

"Karen, remember in the hospital room when you asked me if I could love you, an ordinary girl?"

How could she forget? "I thought you might see something more in me, but I was wrong."

"You weren't wrong. I was afraid to tell you the truth, and I'm sorry for that. When I look at you, I see the woman I love." He held up the ring.

But it was his love for her shining in his eyes, written on his face, tender in his voice that she noticed.

"I've decided that I *am* the man for you. The only one who can cherish you the way you deserve to be." He kissed her hand. "Please. Marry me."

"But I thought—" All she wanted was his love, deep and true. "I thought you didn't love me enough."

"How can that be? I love you with all I have and all I am. I told you before. A man doesn't settle for a woman like you. He gets lucky. Very lucky. I want to spend the rest of my life proving that to you. If you'll have this average, ordinary guy."

All the heartache melted away, and she saw the man before her, offering her his truest love—a once-in-a-lifetime gift. She knew better than to let it slip away.

She'd risk her heart one more time. "Yes. I've wanted to marry you for the longest time. It's like a dream come true."

"*You're* my dream come true." He slipped the diamond on her finger.

It felt so right, his ring on her hand.

Zach pulled her into his arms and brushed her lips

with his. She felt it in his kiss, in the beat of his heart and in the silence that surrounded them.

God had good things in store for them. This was only the beginning.

The back door opened and Michelle's shriek rose into the air. "Did he propose? I can't believe it! Gramma, come see Karen's diamond. Hurry!"

Helen dashed out the door, the two of them clamoring around Karen to look at her ring.

"You're going to have to get used to my sisters," Karen confided in him. "Maybe if we don't tell them which house we buy, they won't be able to find me."

"No good. They'd track you down. It looks like there's no way to escape them."

He loved the way she laughed, the way she fit into his arms, the way she smiled like a promise that said they'd be happy forever.

"My chances for a great-grandbaby are looking better." Gramma beamed. "Zach, welcome to the family."

* * * * *

Dear Reader,

His Hometown Girl is a story very dear to me because I always used to worry as an average and shy girl that I would never find true love. I began to believe it more and more through the years—and that God had forgotten to add romantic love into His plan for my life. Then my good friend began urging me to meet a man she worked with. Since I had my own idea about blind dates, I refused over and over again. Finally I relented. What a surprise. That one dinner changed my life. I learned that God hadn't forgotten me—He'd just been saving the best for last.

I wish you the best and more.

Jillian Hart

Next Month From Steeple Hill®'s

Love Inspired®

Family for Keeps
by
Margaret Daley

Pediatric nurse Tess Morgan's dreams of having a large
family were shattered by a devastating tragedy. But just
when she'd lost all hope for the future, she was drawn
to a strong and tender single father who was no
stranger to grief. Together, could they discover the
healing power of God's love?

**Don't miss
FAMILY FOR KEEPS**

On sale August 2002

Love Inspired®

LIFFK